Making Changes

CW00840189

Mary Grand

Dedication

'Making Changes' is dedicated to my lovely friend Adèle.

Acknowledgements

Many thanks to my husband and Adèle for all their help and support with reading and commenting on these stories before publication. Also to my children for letting me talk through plots and characters when we are out walking. Finally, thank you again to all my fellow cocker spaniel owners on Cockers on Facebook and Cockers Online, the story 'The Right Shoes' is especially for you.

Contents

Page

Holly's Perfect Christmas?

Holly knew that the idea of a 'perfect Christmas' was ridiculous, but she still allowed herself to have dreams. One dream had been to go and stay in a stone cottage in the mountains. Life so far had always made this impossible. However, in August, while everyone else was packing for their summer holidays, it dawned on her that this year it could actually be possible. Of course, it would mean some pretty big concessions from her partner, Gethin. She hesitated: she tried not to ask too much of him. His ex, Sarah, had been, in fact still was, incredibly demanding. Holly put off approaching the subject for weeks.

It was not until one crisp September afternoon, as they walked through Bute Park in Cardiff, that she approached the subject.

'I've been thinking about Christmas–'

'Christmas?' Gethin looked confused. He started to kick the orangey-brown leaves.

'I know for the past few years we've had Sarah, Tom and Lizzy over–'

'Well, Sarah and I did promise Lizzy we would still always have Christmas Day together when we divorced.'

'I know, and maybe your daughter needed it then, but I think it's time for a change.'

Gethin stopped kicking leaves. His eyes widened in horror. 'You weren't thinking of us going to their house, were you? Tom would cope. Sarah is lucky to have married someone so level-headed, but you know what a state she gets in: it would be a nightmare.'

'No. I wasn't going to suggest that.'

Gethin started to scratch his beard. 'What were you thinking, then?'

'I was thinking of us going away somewhere, just you and me.'

'Go away? Leave everyone for Christmas?' Holly saw his eyebrows shoot up.

'Yes.'

'But what about Lizzy?'

'I honestly don't think she'll be that bothered. She's seventeen now. Last year she went round her friend's on Christmas Eve, came home shattered in the morning in time to moan about her presents, then went straight to her room. She didn't spend any time with the family.'

'I know, but–'

'Seriously, Gethin. We will be back for New Year. If Lizzy wants to, she can come to us then. What do you think?'

'I don't know. I should ask her.'

'If you ask her she'll say 'no'. She likes to play you and me off against each other. But this is something I've always wanted to do, and this year it would be really lovely.'

'You're desperate to do this?'

Holly cringed. 'I'm not desperate, but I've always wanted to go away for Christmas. You know, to a cottage in the mountains, but I've never been able to. There were always my parents to care for, and then, of course your, family. Well, this year, I've realised we finally can get away.'

Gethin looked at her intently, as if seeing her for the first time in the conversation. 'This will be your first Christmas without your Dad, won't it?'

Holly shrugged and looked away. 'Yes.'

'I guess it's been hard for you. Your father was ill for so long, and then there were all the late calls from the nursing home, and you had to organise the entire funeral on your own–'

'Well, no-one else was going to.'

'I know, but you were exhausted. It didn't help only taking one day off, and that was for the funeral. I'm sure you should have been entitled to some kind of compassionate leave.'

'So many of my staff were off sick with that bug. I had to keep going.'

Gethin put his arm around her. 'You always do, don't you? You always keep going. Sarah would never cope with a quarter of what you do: you're like Wonder Woman without the Lycra.'

Holly smiled faintly. 'I'm really not, but it would be fun, wouldn't it? For both of us to get away from it all?'

Gethin nodded decisively. 'OK. Let's do it. Let's go away. You're right. Lizzy has all her friends now, and Sarah and Tom should have a Christmas together.'

Before Gethin could get dissuaded by Sarah, Holly quickly searched the internet for a cottage. She had had her heart set on Snowdonia. She had been amazed at how many places had been booked already. It took time, but eventually she found the cottage she wanted. It was rather big, with three bedrooms, but, apart from that, it was perfect. It was an isolated stone farmhouse with a neat slate roof, surrounded by mountains. Inside were flagstones, beams, and large comfortable sofas. There were also the modern things that made life comfortable: a television, wifi, a smart bathroom and a well-equipped kitchen. Added to that, the owners would decorate it for Christmas, and she could put an order in with the local supermarket to have Christmas delivered within hours of their arrival. Holly put down a deposit.

The next big thing was to tell the family. Sarah seemed to accept it. Next came Lizzy, who Gethin wanted to talk to on her own. He was going to an induction for new

3

pupils at the sixth form college with Lizzy, and had decided to mention it to her after that. Holly waited nervously for him to return.

'How did it go?' she asked, pouring him a glass of wine.

'I'm not sure how the college is going to work out. Lizzy has had to compromise on all her choices.'

'Oh dear. I'm sorry. She has her heart set on design. By the way, did you talk to her about Christmas?'

'Oh, yes. Surprisingly, she said she doesn't mind.'

'Really?'

'Yes.'

Holly watched as Gethin gulped down his wine.

'Why do you look so worried then?'

'I'm concerned because all she cares about at the moment is this boy Kane. She's completely obsessed with him.'

'It's her first real boyfriend, isn't it?'

'I know, but why choose him? He's twenty three, no academic qualifications, and he works in that awful pub. I'm sure he serves Lizzy and her friend alcohol. I don't get it. She's so bright and pretty. She could have her choice of boys. Most of all, I'm not happy with the way Kane treats her.'

'I have to say I was surprised when she told me about the way he carries on. He sounds very bossy.'

'He is. You know, he always dictates when they see each other, what they do. She told me he tells her what to wear, and he also told her that men don't like intelligent girls.'

'You are joking! You know she argues for feminism in such a well thought out and passionate way. How come she puts up with this?'

'I don't know. It's awful, and now, because of him, she could fail to get her A Level grades for uni. She needs to settle down now term has started.'

'Sarah will simply have to be firm, make her get down to work.'

Gethin shook his head. 'You know Sarah. She never stands up to Lizzy. She doesn't even seem to be worried about this relationship with Kane. To be honest, I wonder if she's thinking that if Lizzy settled with Kane in Cardiff she wouldn't go off to university.'

'But that's awful. Lizzy's a bright girl.'

'I know. I tried talking to Lizzy tonight about her work, but I'm not sure she was listening and, as I say, Sarah is not backing me up.'

Holly knew there was nothing else she could say, but part of her was relieved that at least they would be still being going away for Christmas.

Things went relatively smoothly for the next few months. Then, in the first week of December, Sarah's husband Tom shocked them all with the news that he had been offered promotion to a new job in Newcastle. He was a senior nurse practitioner in Cardiff, but he had secretly been for an interview for Group Nurse Director, in Newcastle. Now, to his amazement and delight, he had been offered the post. As Sarah had not worked for some time and Lizzy was very unhappy in her sixth form college, Tom saw no good reason why they shouldn't all move from Cardiff to Newcastle in the New Year. However, it was not that simple.

Sarah had been straight on the phone to Gethin, who in turn relayed it all to Holly. He came off the phone white-faced and exhausted.

'Tom really should have discussed this interview with Sarah. She and Lizzy are in shock,' he said.

'I guess so. Maybe he didn't want to worry her until he knew if he'd got the job. Sarah does worry a lot.'

'I suppose so. Anyway, Lizzy has gone crazy and is completely refusing to go.'

'I suppose it's a big move for her. Mind you, she hates her courses at the college.'

'I know and, to give him his due, Tom has checked out sixth forms in Newcastle. He's found a fantastic course which ties in with Newcastle fashion week. Even Lizzy said it looked OK.'

'Is she worried about leaving friends?'

'Not particularly. Her closest friend moved away in the summer–'

'So what is it?'

'It's Kane. I was hoping that would have fizzled out by now, but if anything it is more intense.'

'Oh dear. That's hard.'

'It is.'

Gethin started scratching his chin through his beard. His eyebrows were knitted together. 'What do you think about the move?' Holly asked gently, 'Would you mind Lizzy going all that way?'

'In some ways, but I think it could be good for Lizzy and, after all, she'll be going to uni in a few years. And there are direct flights between Cardiff and Newcastle.'

'What about Sarah? I know she can still phone you from Newcastle, but she demands to see you a lot.'

'Maybe a bit of distance won't be a bad thing.' Gethin gave a weak smile.

'So the only problem really is Lizzy not wanting to leave Kane?'

'Exactly, and Sarah refuses to confront her. She is saying now that Tom shouldn't take the job; she'll never force Lizzy to do anything, and she won't leave her.'

Holly sighed. She knew there was something she should offer. Reluctantly, she said, 'I suppose Lizzy could live with us for the rest of her sixth form–'

Gethin shook his head. 'Sarah already suggested that. Lizzy says she has to live with her Mum.'

Holly tutted in frustration. 'This is daft. Tom should be able to take this job. Sarah should stop letting Lizzy mess them all around like this.'

'I know, but honestly I can't see Sarah fighting Lizzy.'

'But what about Tom? Surely she can see his point of view?'

'Gosh. I don't know. I do think Sarah loves him, but Lizzy is her life.'

The phone calls and meetings between Sarah and Gethin went on all week. It was during this time that Holly was told that inspectors were coming to her school the following Monday.

The night before, Sunday evening, with a pile of paperwork spread around the dining table, she had a rare moan to Gethin about work.

'Bloody inspectors,' she said, banging her pen on the table. 'Why come two weeks before the end of the Christmas term? They know that work at this point in the term normally takes second place to the Christmas play and parties. Now the staff have to prepare lessons and no-one knows how they're going to fit in rehearsals. They have to shout at someone, so, of course, as Head, they take it out on me.'

Gethin came over to her. 'It's not fair, love. You all work so hard.'

She felt his arms around her shoulders, warm and comforting. Having never lived with a partner before, she had been nervous about them living together, but the past two years with Gethin had been some of the most content she had known. She had even wondered about them getting married, but they had never discussed it. Somehow, Sarah and Lizzy still seemed to occupy a lot of Gethin's time.

Holly had met Gethin at a party not long after the break-up of his marriage of fourteen years. Despite missing his daughter, Lizzy, Gethin had not looked shattered, but rather had the look of someone stepping on to dry land after being caught in a long hard storm at sea. He was a man in search of calm and tranquillity, which Holly understood. They both had demanding jobs in Cardiff, she as a head teacher and he as a senior social worker. When Holly moved in with Gethin, she worked hard at creating a home that was as organised and as peaceful as possible. The only real source of stress came from Sarah who, despite having left Gethin and now being married to Tom, frequently rang and demanded his time. Of course, they still had Lizzy, but Sarah's phone calls were usually about the drama in her own life.

Everything with Sarah was a crisis, be it health, relationships or the whole range of minor irritations everyone has to live with. Sarah reacted to the woman in the post office telling her that she had addressed a package the wrong way in the same way as someone crashing into her car: there was no sense of perspective. Whenever Tom refused to react sufficiently to his wife's outbursts, Sarah rang Gethin.

It had always been frustrating for Holly, but this last week, with the drama of Tom's new job and possible move, things had reached a new height of hysteria. It was in the middle of this that Holly had been told about the school inspection. She had tried not to worry Gethin, but she was extremely anxious. As Gethin stroked her brown curls he said, 'I'll make us some decent coffee, and toast some crumpets: lots of butter and jam.'

'Thanks. That would be great.'

Gethin stood up but, before he got to the kitchen, his phone rang. Holly knew who it was, and saw him wander into the conservatory. He pulled the sliding door across but, if she listened closely, she could hear what he was saying. 'Oh hi, Sarah. How are things?'

Holly tried not to get wound up, but found herself gripping her pen tighter and grinding her teeth. In the same way that she knew you should never pick a scab, she knew she shouldn't listen, but she couldn't resist. As they crept closer to Christmas, she became increasingly anxious that Sarah might find a way to sabotage her plans to go away, and she had a horrible feeling that this new crisis could be the thing that would do it.

Holly could hear the murmur of voices as Gethin tried to reason with Sarah.

'It could be good for Lizzy. Try to be firm.'

Even from the living room, Holly could hear the echoes of hysteria down the phone. She heard Gethin say, 'Well, Kane could still see her if he saved up. Honestly, I would like Lizzy to have some time apart from him.'

Gethin seemed to go quiet for a long time. Sarah was obviously in full swing about something. When he did speak, Gethin's voice had changed. Now it was tense and strained. 'I see. I didn't realise. They have good hospitals and doctors up there. I am sure they would take good care of you. No, of course.'

There was silence. Then, as Holly listened closely, she heard something that made her shiver.

'I don't know about that. I told you, it's difficult. Holly has Christmas all planned.'

Holly slammed down her pen, and only just stopped herself from running into the conservatory and grabbing the phone. Sarah was not going to ruin this Christmas; no way. Soon after that, she heard the phone call finish. Gethin came back into the room. He looked exhausted, and was scratching his beard hard.

Holly quickly picked up her pen, and looked down at her work.

'Gosh, things go from bad to worse,' he said.

'Mmm–'

'Well, you know Lizzy's very upset about the move to Newcastle–'

Holly looked up. 'I know, but she'll get used to it, and, as you said, it would be a good thing to move her away from Kane.'

Gethin sat down next to her at the dining table where she was working. 'Mm, yes. It's more difficult than I realised, though. Sarah has just been telling me she has been going for a lot of blood tests. The consultant wants her in for more tests. I'm not sure it's the right time for her to be moving.'

'Really?' Holly felt a pang of guilt. 'What's the matter?'

'They think it's her liver.'

'Oh dear. What does Tom say?'

'Apparently, he refuses to take it seriously. She asked me to talk to him.'

'But surely he'd know if it's serious. Is it possible she is exaggerating?'

'I don't think so. She was in tears.'

'But they do have health care in Newcastle.'

'But she's under a good consultant here: someone she trusts. So, what with that and Lizzy, I'm not sure now that Tom shouldn't re-think things.'

'But you thought they should go. And job offers like this don't come around often.'

'But Tom should be putting them first.'

Holly shook her head. 'They need to talk more about this together.'

Gethin looked at her directly. 'Yes, I agree, and that's part of why I want to ask you something. I know it's a big favour–' Holly screwed up her eyes in a very headteacherly way. Gethin scratched his beard nervously. 'It's about Christmas,' he added.

She raised her eyebrows. 'I hope you're not thinking about asking me to cancel the holiday.'

'No. I wasn't going to ask that.'

Holly sighed with relief. 'Good. What is it, then?'

She had relaxed too soon. 'The thing is, Sarah asked if they could come to the cottage with us.' Holly heard the words rush out: obviously Gethin thought it was like taking off a plaster, and would hurt less if done quickly.

'Oh God, no,' Holly exclaimed. 'No way.'

'Sarah thinks a change of scenery would be good for them all. She and Tom could talk properly. You know, their house is in chaos at the moment. All the dust is making her feel awful, but Tom insists on having this work done.'

'The kitchen was in a bad way and, if they do move, they need it more presentable to sell.'

'Whatever, the state of the house is getting on top of Sarah,' continued Gethin, 'and, if Sarah could get a complete break, maybe it would give Tom time to think as well.'

Holly saw the knuckles of Gethin's hands go white as he clasped them together. She felt sorry for him. 'You know, it's their marriage. They need to sort it out.'

'Yes, but I have to help if I can. I have to think of Lizzy.'

'But Lizzy is growing up–'

Gethin unclenched his hands and breathed deeply. 'It wouldn't be the end of the world for them to come, would it? Sarah loves Snowdonia. She needs a holiday, and we do have three bedrooms. Please. I'm really worried about Sarah, and it would give me space to talk to Lizzy. If they were to go, I will be seeing a lot less of her.'

Holly looked at Gethin, miserably torn by all the demands being made on him.

'Lizzy might not want to leave Kane for all that time at Christmas.'

'She says as long as there is wifi she will come. That would be a good thing as well: get her away from him for a few days.'

'But Tom won't want to come, will he?'

'He doesn't mind. He said he fancies a break.'

'Hang on. So everyone has discussed this apart from me?'

Gethin tried to smile. 'Well, yes. I didn't think you would mind too much, but–'

Holly slumped in her seat.

'I'm sorry. Maybe it's too much to ask of you–' Gethin was saying.

His reasonableness combined with how wretched he looked made her feel guilty.

'I'm sorry,' she said, but she knew there was weakness in her voice. Gethin picked it up.

'It wouldn't have to be the whole week, just a night or two–'

'What do you mean?'

Gethin's face lit up. 'Say they came on the Saturday before Christmas and leave the day after Boxing Day?'

Holly looked at the calendar on her phone. 'That would mean they would arrive the same day as us, the Saturday, and then leave on the Wednesday.'

'Giving us the rest of the week to ourselves.'

Holly bit the end of her pen. Of course, she could refuse, but they both knew now that she wouldn't. The battle was lost. 'You say just a few nights? Well, I suppose, if they went on the Wednesday morning–'

Gethin hugged her. 'You're an angel.'

'If you mean like Ellie, our Angel Gabriel, who I saw whacking a shepherd in rehearsals, I think you could be right.'

He laughed, then said, 'Sarah asked me to pop round. Is that alright? Tom and Lizzy are out. She's very worried about everything. She has more blood tests tomorrow, and thinking about Christmas will cheer her up.'

'OK,' said Holly. She heard the front door slam, and went to make herself the cup of coffee and crumpets.

By the time Gethin and Holly were driving up to Snowdonia early on the Saturday morning before Christmas, Holly had become reconciled to the new arrangements. The school inspection had gone well; she was relaxed, felt she could handle anything. It was a bright icy day. The back seat was covered in carefully wrapped presents. Holly put on some music: this was her favourite Christmas CD. Every year she saved it for Christmas week. She had had time to become reconciled to the next few days and she was determined to make the best of it. The order she had put into the supermarket had cost a fortune, but she had ordered the best of everything.

When they stopped off at a pub for lunch, they noticed the sky was heavy and grey.

'Looks like snow,' seemed to be the consensus of the people in the pub, and they all looked up at the sky with a sense of foreboding and excitement.

'Bookies have stopped taking bets on a white Christmas,' said the barman. 'Let's face it, it's a done deal.' Holly didn't understand why he looked quite so miserable, until he said, 'We're booked out for Christmas Day. Don't want people not turning up because of the snow. You know what people are like: a few flakes and they think the end of the world has come.'

'Well, they'll have to come. They won't have any food in,' said Gethin, reasonably.

'Don't you believe it. I bet all their fridges are packed to the gunnels. Have you seen the way people shop for Christmas? It's as if they're preparing for a nuclear war.'

Gethin grinned at Holly: this man refused to be cheered up. They sat down and enjoyed their lunch of sausages and mash in thick onion gravy. It was filling and comforting, and they couldn't resist pudding. They sat chatting contentedly by the log fire in the pub with little inclination to go back out into the cold.

By the time they finally came out, the sky had darkened and Holly needed to put on the headlights. Snow started to fall and, as they came off the major road, the driving became more treacherous. Slowly, a new, intense darkness enveloped the car. Holly's vision was eventually restricted to the area illuminated by her headlights, and these showed thick patches of ice, and a smattering of snow. She decided that white Christmases were far more fun observed through the window of a snug, centrally-heated house than a freezing car windscreen.

Eventually they arrived at a village. It had more shops than Holly would have expected. There were tearooms, an antique shop and a small supermarket. All were decorated and busy. They drove past the shops, and turned right on to a rough track. The driving was difficult, uneven and icy. Holly was glad when they eventually reached the cottage.

There was a light on by the front door, and she could see a holly wreath on the front door. She got out, and found the key, as instructed, under a metal pail to the left of the door. Pushing open the door, she instantly smelt the sweet pine of the tree. Someone had obviously come in very recently to prepare the cottage. At one end a wood burner glowed. Next to it, the Christmas tree was lit up with a hundred tiny, soft cream lights. Switching on the main lights, she looked around at the cosy room. At one end was the kitchen area. The rest was a large living room. The floor was flagstones but there were warming rugs and large comfy sofas. On the coffee table a Christmas card from the owners greeted them with "Nadolig Llawen". A large plate of homemade mince pies and a bottle of port stood next to it. It was like something from a film, the perfect setting for Christmas.

'Gosh. It's wonderful. It's exactly how I imagined it,' Holly whispered.

Gethin put down the first lot of bags. He took her in his arms, and kissed her. 'Happy Christmas.'

'And Happy Christmas to you,' Holly replied.

They brought the rest of the things in, and shut out the freezing cold, then through the window Holly saw headlights coming up the drive, and realised it was a delivery van.

'Good timing. Christmas has arrived.'

Holly let in the delivery man carrying the green boxes of food and provisions.

'Bet you're glad to be snug in here,' he said. 'More snow on the way.'

'I'm relieved you made it,' said Holly. 'We'd have been really stuck if you hadn't.'

After she had quickly emptied the boxes, the man left, and Holly began to organise the kitchen. She had tried to think of everyone's preferences when doing the order, had even ordered vegetarian alternatives just in case Lizzy had decided once more to go veggie.

'I think I'll open this,' said Gethin, picking up the bottle of port.

'Good idea.'

They found glasses and stood in front of the Christmas tree drinking the port. Holly realised it seemed a long time since she had seen Gethin look so relaxed. If only–

As if reading her mind, Gethin said, 'You know, I wish it was just you and me now. Life gets so complicated with Sarah.'

Holly smiled, but didn't say anything.

'You know, I think we should go up and choose the best room, don't you?' added Gethin. Grinning, Holly put down her glass. They went upstairs. Holly knew immediately which room she wanted. There was a king-sized bed with sprigged flowers on the duvet that matched the curtains. And it looked over the front of the house. The moon was shining down outside on the ever-thickening snow.

'Gosh. I hope the others are alright,' said Holly, ever practical.

Gethin put his arms around her. 'Well, you never know. Maybe they'll turn back and it will be just you and me. I think I could cope with that.' He pulled Holly towards him. 'I do love you so much, Holly. I'm sorry if this isn't quite what you planned, but you'll be alright, won't you? I mean, you always cope, don't you?' He glanced out of the window. They both noticed headlights coming up the drive. 'Hell, they're here.'

They went downstairs. Holly headed for the door. She held it ajar, not wanting the cold and hot air to be exchanged. As she stood wondering why they were taking so long to get out of the car Holly heard her phone 'ping' a text. She took it out of her pocket. Glancing, she didn't recognise the number, and wondered briefly if it was to do with school. She opened the text, but frowned when she saw what it was: this was nothing to do with school. Before she could say anything to Gethin, she saw the car doors open.

Tom, always friendly, walked ahead of Sarah and Lizzy, but his smile seemed tight and his eyes were screwed up. 'Gethin,' he said. 'Good to see you.' He turned to Holly. The frozen smile relaxed slightly. 'You look fantastic,' he said, and hugged her.

Sarah came next. Very small, petite. Long fair hair tumbled over the shoulders of her smart camel woollen coat. However, the expensively made-up eyes were nervously blinking and she was biting her bright red lips. Today her eyes darted around. She looked past Holly to Tom, then at Gethin, who was smiling reassuringly at her. 'Are you OK? Good journey?'

'God, no. I really thought at one point we would die. It's horrendous out there. We could have got stranded, or driven into a ditch.'

Holly rolled her eyes. Gethin said, 'Well, you're here now, and Holly has taken care of everything.'

Lizzy walked towards them, her head bowed, as she was busy texting.

'Hi,' said Holly.

Lizzy looked up blankly. 'Oh, hi,' then to her father, 'My phone is working, thank God. Do you know the password for the wifi?'

'We'll look it up in the house file.'

Holly turned to Tom, who was holding cases. 'We thought Gethin and I could have the front room, with Lizzy next to us. You and Sarah can go in the back room. It's ensuite.'

'Great, thanks.'

They all started taking cases upstairs. There was little chatting. Gethin took refuge in working out how to use the sky box on the television.

Holly went upstairs to their bedroom and shut the door. She took out her phone, and looked again at the text. It was a photograph that showed Gethin and Sarah sitting at a local pub. That didn't particularly bother her: she knew Gethin sometimes went for a drink with Sarah out of the house if he needed to talk about Lizzy. Slightly more unsettling however was the message that came with it: *'They belong together. You should never have come between them.'* Who ever had sent it?

Holly checked through her address book: she definitely had no record of the number. Her initial reaction was that it must have been sent by Lizzy on a friend's phone. That didn't worry her too much. It was just childish, but she decided she would mention it to Gethin. The text had an unpleasant feel to it that made her uneasy.

17

Holly went downstairs, but found that Gethin had now settled himself down to sorting out Lizzy's wifi so that she could use her laptop. She realised she would have to wait to talk to him. Always finding comfort in activity, Holly offered to make the evening meal. She set to making a large chilli with rice; she put on the radio and listened to Christmas songs. By the time she had finished cooking Lizzy had taken her laptop upstairs to message Kane. Holly asked Gethin to go and let her know the meal was ready.

He returned quickly. 'Sorry, she can't come yet. She and Kane are having some kind of heavy talk.'

'Not again,' said Tom. 'She's only seventeen. This relationship is far too intense. It's another reason why we should move.'

'You don't understand how much Kane means to Lizzy,' protested Sarah.

Holly cringed and looked down; she hated rows.

'This is just an adolescent crush. You should see that,' said Tom.

Sarah turned around. 'She doesn't want to move. I won't make her.'

'But it's only because of this boy, and that will never last. She hates the sixth form. She hasn't even got a strong bunch of friends. In Newcastle, you know, she's been making contact with some people up there on Facebook.'

'How do you know that?'

'She's friends on there with someone's kid at work. He told me. She's been talking to people who go to some design group up there.'

'That doesn't mean anything,' responded Sarah.

'Shall we start on the meal before it gets cold?' suggested Holly.

They all sat round the table. Holly opened a bottle of wine and started to fill the glasses.

'Not for me,' said Sarah in a loud voice. 'I don't want to spend Christmas in intensive care.'

Holly poured herself a large glass of wine. Lizzy, red eyed, appeared from the stairs.

'I've made chilli, your favourite,' said Holly, but she was ignored.

'What's up darling?' asked Sarah. 'You look terrible.'

'You know what's wrong,' said Lizzy. 'Kane won't do a long distance relationship. In fact, we have just been talking and made a decision. If you go with Tom to Newcastle, I shall move in with Kane.'

'I don't think so,' interrupted Gethin quietly, but he was soon drowned out by Sarah screaming hysterically, 'Oh my God. No. No way.' Sarah turned on Tom. 'See: we can't go now.'

Holly watched Lizzy lift her head a little higher in triumph at the reaction.

'I think it's the perfect solution,' Lizzy said.

'You'd hate living with him,' said Tom. 'We know where he lives. It's grotty, and he shares with three other lads who you can't stand. You won't even go round there for a meal.'

'Well, I'd have to get used to it,' responded Lizzy. 'Kane's right. You have no right to make me move. I'll be thousands of miles from him and all my friends.'

'It's a simple flight away. You'll be coming down to see your Dad. Your friends can come and stay and, anyway, you'll make new friends.'

Lizzy glared at Tom. 'You are being completely selfish. You're completely stressing Mum out.'

'You're the one stressing your mother.'

'No. That's not true,' said Sarah tearfully. 'Lizzy has every right to expect her mother to stick by her. I can see how much Kane means to her, but there is no way she is moving in with a boy at the age of seventeen. Even you should see we have to stay.'

'She won't go and live with him,' said Tom, exasperated. 'She'll have forgotten all about Kane in a few weeks.'

'I won't,' shouted Lizzy. 'I love him, and if I go I'll lose him, and I'd never forgive you for that.'

'You're only young.'

'But I know when I'm in love.'

'I've said you could live with me and Holly,' interrupted Gethin.

Lizzy looked at him as if he had suggested living in the local tip.

'And I said no way. I want to live with my Mum. I love you, Dad, but me and Mum are very close. She understands me.'

Holly felt sorry for Gethin to be dismissed so easily. Lizzy, though, seemed completely unaware of how she was hurting her father. She was too busy preparing the final sting. 'Of course, if you and Mum hadn't split up this would never have happened.'

'Lizzy, where on earth is this coming from?' asked Gethin, shocked.

Holly thought about the text on her phone. She was sure then that it was from Lizzy. She looked over at Gethin, who was clenching his fists, but he spoke quietly.

'We've talked about this plenty of times, Lizzy. Me and Mum were not happy together. Your Mum has married Tom, and Holly means everything to me.'

'No, she doesn't.'

'She does.'

'But me and Mum–'

'I love you both very much. You know that–'

'Well, Mum needs you more than Holly. I was thinking. If you got back with Mum, she'd stay in Cardiff. Nothing would have to change.'

Tom coughed. 'Excuse me interrupting, Lizzy,' he said, with more than a hint of sarcasm, 'Your mother and I are married. That is not changing. You are the one making your mother miserable. If you weren't being so damn difficult she'd be fine.'

Holly sat watching them all. It was like a TV soap: all shouting outrageous things; no one listening to each other. With a final glare at Holly, Lizzy got up and stormed upstairs. Holly frowned, and wondered why she was suddenly being blamed for this. It was as bad as school.

They all sat very quietly, avoiding eye contact.

'I'm sorry. She didn't mean it,' Gethin said to Holly.

'I think she did, actually.'

Then, much to Holly's surprise, Gethin said to Tom, 'Is there any way you could postpone this move, say, for a year or two; get Lizzy through her A levels down here?'

'Of course not. I will lose the job, and will probably never be offered another one like it. To be honest, I don't think this has anything to do with you, Gethin.'

'Taking my daughter to Newcastle has a great deal to do with me. And then there's Sarah. She's not well.'

Tom pursed his lips, and shook his head. 'Lizzy will be going to university soon. That could be anywhere, and as for Sarah being ill–'

'Yes, and you should be looking after her,' said Gethin.

'Don't tell me how to treat my wife.' Tom stood up and leant forward, confronting Gethin. 'You know, I reckon you like Sarah coming to you, playing the hero, but you need to butt out of our marriage. I don't know how Holly puts up with it.'

'Holly doesn't mind. She's not needy like Sarah.' He looked at Holly and smiled, but Holly didn't smile back.

Tom scowled. 'I'm serious. You're a good bloke, Gethin, but you need to live your own life now.'

Gethin turned red. 'That's ridiculous. Tom, before you met Sarah you had never had family or responsibilities.

Well, now you have. You have to start looking after them, then maybe I wouldn't have to be constantly on call with them.'

Tom grabbed an opened bottle of wine, then his coat. 'I won't stay here to be lectured by you.' He opened the front door, letting a blast of cold air into the room, and slammed it behind him.

Gethin put his head in his hands. 'What a nightmare.' He poked his food with his fork, but then threw it aside. 'It's no good. I'd better go and talk to Tom. This is stupid.'

Gethin put his coat on and followed him.

'I'll have a lie down. I'm exhausted,' said Sarah. She pushed aside her untouched food, sighed deeply, and walked wearily upstairs. Holly started to clear the table. No-one had eaten much. Sarah hadn't looked too well but, for all that, Holly felt peeved that, as always, she was left with the mundane task of clearing up alone.

When she had finished, she sat by the tree. It was very quiet. All she could hear was the crackling of the logs in the wood burner. The heat warmed her face. She had closed her eyes, and was feeling like a cat luxuriating in the warmth, when Gethin returned.

'I couldn't find Tom.'

'He can't have gone far.'

'Well I don't know. It's freezing out there. Maybe I'd better go and talk to Lizzy.'

'Take it gently. We don't want any more rows.'

Gethin went upstairs. Holly heard him knock on Lizzy's door.

Holly looked over at the tree, and wondered if anyone else had even noticed it. She sniffed hard. Maybe she had been foolish to think that she could have some kind of idyllic Christmas. She touched the pine branches, which released their perfume. She breathed in deeply. Maybe she should just savour these special moments. Then her phone pinged. She looked down: it was another text from that number. Holly didn't want to look at it, but knew she had to.

'*You are making everyone miserable. You're an f***in home wrecker. You heard Gethin. He loves them. You don't need him. Let them be a family again. By the way, she hates chilli. You don't know her at all.*'

Holly was shocked by the language and forcefulness of the text. Clasping her phone, she walked quickly upstairs. She knocked briskly on Lizzy's door and went in. Lizzy was sitting on her bed cuddling a teddy. Gethin sat next to her. They both looked at her, surprised.

Holly handed her phone to Gethin, showing him the texts.

'Who on earth would send them? There's no name.'

'It must be someone here. Look again at the second one. It's someone who was here at the meal.'

Gethin read it again. 'Oh no. I'm so sorry, love.'

Holly looked from Gethin to Lizzy. He gave an infinitessimal nod.

'OK. Leave your phone with me,' he said.

Holly nodded back, turned, left the room, and went back downstairs.

She poured herself a glass of port and sat next to the tree. At that moment Tom returned. His jet black hair had a smattering of snow. He thumped his feet, rather harder than necessary, on the doormat.

'You on your own?' His words were slurred. Holly noticed that the bottle was empty.

'Gethin's talking to Lizzy. Sarah's having a lie down.'

Tom took off his coat, threw it on the back of a chair, and fell into the chair.

'God, what a mess,' he exclaimed.

'It's all very difficult.'

'Why does Sarah make everything so hard? If she put her foot down with Lizzy there would be no problem, but she never has. She always takes her side against me. They have these long secret chats in Lizzy's bedroom. I never know what they are talking about.'

'They've always been close.'

'I know, and I've made loads of concessions to that, but, you know, I've just about had enough.'

Holly felt alarmed. 'What do you mean?'

'Gethin was right. I was a bachelor, and a very happy one. No responsibilities. You know how long I've waited for a job like this to come along? It's not just the money, though heaven knows it would be wonderful. I'd be on double what I earn now. It would be so interesting. Sarah should know that, but everything has to be about her. It's exhausting.'

'I think Gethin found it all a bit much.'

'He says that. I can't help wondering, though, whether he doesn't miss being needed. Maybe that's why he lets Sarah go running to him all the time. I don't know. Maybe she was better off with him.'

Holly frowned. 'I don't think so.'

Tom shook his head. 'Well, I can't help thinking that if that's what she wants, maybe she'd better get on with it.'

Holly watched. Tom was staring blankly into the log burner. He had obviously forgotten she was there. She was about to say that she was involved with this as well, when he seemed to sink back into the chair and closed his eyes. There was no point in talking to him.

Holly quietly got up and went upstairs. Gethin was not in their room. He was still in with Lizzy. Holly changed into her nightdress, climbed into bed, and found her book to read. However, she held it in front of her, not reading the words. Soon Gethin appeared.

'Lizzy alright?' she asked.

'She's all over the place.' He handed Holly her phone.

'Did you ask her about the texts?'

24

'I did. She says she didn't send them. You know, I believe her.'

'Why? Because she told you she didn't do it?'

'Well, yes. I usually know when she's lying, and she seemed genuinely shocked by them.'

Holly shrugged. He would think that, wouldn't he?

'Anyway, she couldn't have sent the second one.'

'What do you mean?'

'Think about it. It was sent while I was talking to her. She didn't have her phone the whole time I was with her.'

'Oh, you're sure?'

'I am.'

'But it talked about the chilli. It had to be someone here. That means Sarah or Tom.'

'That doesn't seem very likely.'

'Tom was talking to me just now. Granted he was pretty drunk, but he does seem fed up with Sarah at the moment. Maybe he wants you to take her back. He could go off and take this job then.'

'You make him sound very fickle.'

'Oh, I don't know. It's a right mess.'

Gethin put his arm around Holly.

'Listen; you make it sound like I'm here for the taking.'

'Well, Sarah always finds you ready to listen. Sometimes I think you talk more to her than to me.'

Gethin's eyebrows shot up. 'It's because she needs me and, to be honest, I've always been worried about losing Lizzy. To keep in touch with Lizzy I guess I've felt I had to keep in touch with Sarah. I certainly don't want to get back with Sarah. Honestly, I really want her to stay with Tom.'

'Really?'

Gethin held her closer. 'This isn't like you. You know how much you mean to me.'

'Tom said he thought you liked to be needed. You know, I need you as well.'

Gethin kissed her gently. 'You know, that's the first time you have ever said that.'

Holly shrugged, and looked down. 'It's these texts. They've unnerved me.'

'Look, things have been tense tonight, but it got things out in the open. I'm sure they'll stop now. Just think: tomorrow is Christmas Eve. Let's make it a good one, eh?'

Gethin kissed her cheek, and rolled over away from her. To Holly's amazement he was asleep within minutes.

Holly lay on her back but couldn't sleep: too many things were racing around her mind. She heard a thump on the stairs, followed by whispered swearing, and guessed Tom was going to bed. She continued to lie there, listening to Gethin quietly snoring. He usually slept well. He was very good at putting worries into boxes. She guessed it was why he coped so well with his job. She drifted off to sleep, but woke in the early hours very thirsty. She crept out of bed and downstairs, using her phone as a flashlight. It all seemed so much darker than home: no street lights or buildings lending them light.

She went straight to the kitchen, but heard a noise from the sofa. She shone her light around, and to her surprise saw Sarah, with an empty wine glass in her hand.

'Are you alright?' Holly asked.

Sarah put down the glass quickly. 'I wasn't drinking. This must have been Tom's.'

It was obvious she was lying. Surely she wasn't allowed to drink?

'I couldn't sleep. I came down for some water,' said Holly. 'Shall I pour you a glass?'

'Thanks.'

Sarah came over to her. Holly glanced down at her phone. She wondered if she should say something about the texts, but was worried about Sarah's reaction waking the household. Instead, she handed Sarah the glass.

'Good night, then,' Sarah said and, ghost-like, went back upstairs. Bemused, Holly watched her. Sarah knew how to make leaving a room into 'an exit', conveying this time fragility and vulnerability. Maybe Tom and Gethin liked that. Holly knew plenty of women who played that part. Maybe they had learned from a young age that it was the only way to get what they wanted, but it had never been Holly's way. She returned to her own room.

There was a strange light in the room the next morning. Holly got out of bed and opened the curtains.

'It's been snowing again, Gethin. Come and see. It's like magic.'

Gethin crawled out of bed, and stood next to her. 'Wow, miles of snow. Incredible. Glad we don't need to get anywhere.'

'I'm jolly pleased it's not a school day. I hate all that worry about whether I should close the school. I'm lucky I can get in easily, like most of the children, but half the staff live in the back of beyond. I think some of the parents think I should run the school single-handed.'

'Not today, anyway. It's Christmas Eve, and we're on holiday,' he said, adding with a winning smile, 'I don't suppose you fancy cooking breakfast?'

'OK. Yes, we need to make the most of this. We could build a snowman later.'

Gethin laughed. Holly put on her dressing gown and headed downstairs.

Tom was already there, making up the wood burner.

'Amazing out there, isn't it?' he said, looking remarkably bright.

'You look very awake.'

He grinned. 'Sorry about last night. I probably spoke a lot of nonsense. Anyway, today's a new day, and Christmas Eve at that.'

'Bacon and eggs?'

'I'll say.'

It all seemed so normal now. The night before seemed suddenly like some horrible dream.

'Shall I do some for Sarah?' Holly asked.

'Oh, no. She's not really a breakfast person at the moment.'

'Is something the matter with her? She doesn't look well.'

Tom looked away, but then Gethin came down for breakfast. He seemed happy and relaxed. He tucked into his food. When he had finished he said, 'Right Holly, Tom and I will tidy up. You do what you want for a bit.'

She smiled. 'OK. You know, I think I'll get dressed and go outside. I always love to be the first to make footprints in the snow.' She threw on some clothes and wellingtons and went outside.

The sun was shining on the snow. It was crunchy: snowman-making snow. The sky was blue-grey, but promised more snow to come. At the moment, the snow only just covered the foot of her wellingtons. It was very quiet, the snow dampening all sounds. Holly felt like she had landed in Narnia, and expected the fawn, Mr Tumnus, to come out from behind a tree. She saw a robin really close by singing as if he was posing for a Christmas card. It was idyllic.

Then her phone pinged. She took a glove off and reached into her pocket, wishing now that she had left it in the house. It was just habit, though: when you leave the house, you take phone, keys, and purse.

It was "the number". Holly frowned as she opened the text. 'The best Christmas present you could give Sarah and Lilly is to give back Gethin.' Holly frowned. It quickly went through her mind to wonder who Lilly was, but she assumed that the sender had misspelt Lizzy, or got in a muddle with predictive text.

The words tore up the beauty of the morning. She couldn't bear it anymore. Holly stomped through the snow and threw open the front door. Gethin and Tom were still at the dining table, and looked deeply engrossed in a conversation.

'You said they'd stop,' she shouted at Gethin, holding out her phone, 'but I just got another one.'

Gethin and Tom came over to her. She showed Gethin the phone, and Tom read the text over his shoulder.

'Was it you, Tom?' she asked quietly, realising her voice was shaking and she was close to tears.

He shook his head. 'No, of course not. I love Sarah. I don't want my marriage to end.'

'But last night–'

'That was the drink. I do get fed up but I'd never leave Sarah. Anyway, I wouldn't send an anonymous text. It's so childish and mean.'

'Someone did,' she said; then she realised that Gethin was looking away. He seemed preoccupied.

'Is something else the matter?' she asked.

'It's nothing.'

'What is it? You two were looking very serious when I came in. is it Sarah? What's the matter with her?'

'I've been so stupid.' Gethin looked over at Tom. 'You should explain.'

Tom gave a deep sigh. 'This is embarrassing. The thing is, I went with Sarah for the last appointment. She hadn't been letting me go to anything, which was odd. I knew she's been to path lab a lot, and I was getting worried. So, when I knew she was seeing the consultant, I just turned up. She couldn't stop me going in with her.'

'Why didn't she want you to go with her? I thought she was cross that you weren't taking her seriously.'

'Look, I had been trying to reassure her, that's all, but I was starting to get worried.'

'And–'

'The consultant told us that the blood tests were all clear. The only reason she has been for so many blood tests was because she kept refusing to let them do it.'

'Oh no. When was this appointment?'

'The day before we came here.'

'She's been making it all up?'

'Yes.'

'You must have been really angry.'

'I was upset. We had quite a row.'

'And why was she doing it?'

'She says she felt stuck in a corner. She'd told Lizzy she wouldn't leave her, but she also wants to be with me. It was her way of making me stay.'

Holly scowled. 'That's awful: to lie about being ill. How dare she?'

Tom sighed. 'She plays games. I know that. I was cross when she did that thing about the drinking yesterday. She promised me she'd stop pretending to be ill. We had words about it this morning.'

Holly looked at her phone. 'So is this one of her games as well?'

Tom shook his head. 'I don't think she would do that.'

Holly threw her phone on to the sofa in exasperation.

'She will always win, won't she? People like me, we just carry on, and she gets all the concessions made to her.' She turned to Gethin. 'You're just as bad. I'm tired of trying to fit in with you. You give her all the time and energy that you should be giving me.'

'You never complain.'

'No, but I shouldn't have to, Gethin. You should know I need to be looked after. Coming here was the one thing I have asked for, and you ruined it.'

30

'Oh, love. I'm so sorry.'

Holly found herself shaking. She felt sick and out of control. Suddenly, months of stored up tears burned her face. She gulped for breath. Gethin put his arms around her, and held her tightly.

'What's going on?' a voice asked.

Holly sniffed hard, and looked up to see Lizzy.

'My God, Holly. You never cry,' said Lizzy. 'Whatever has happened?'

Gethin held out the phone. 'She got another text this morning.'

Holly thought it sounded a decent explanation for her outburst.

Lizzy took the phone and read the text. She gasped. 'Oh my God. What a prick.'

They all looked at her. She blushed.

'What do you mean?' Gethin asked.

'I'm sorry, but it's Kane. I'm sure of it. Lilly is his pet name for me. No-one else calls me that. He must have got your number off my phone, and used a friend's or something. He took that photograph. He was out with some friends and saw you. He took it on his phone and showed it to me.'

'But why?' asked Holly

'He said he thought that you and Mum should get back together. He said then I would be able to stay in Cardiff with him.'

'Really?' said Holly.

'Yes. It shows how much he loves me, doesn't it?' Holly heard the desperation in Lizzy's voice.

'To be honest, Lizzy, I think it's a bit controlling,' said Gethin. 'You're a bright girl. You'll want to go to university one day, and he'll have to face up to that.'

Lizzy didn't answer directly. 'I'm going up for a bit.'

Finally, Sarah seemed to have become aware of the drama and came downstairs. Tom told her about the texts.

'Kane did that?' said Sarah.

'Yes,' said Gethin. 'I told you he's not good for Lizzy.'

Sarah shook her head. 'I suppose you're right. Sending texts and taking photos like that–'

'Exactly. She needs time away from him. Tom is right.'

'But she doesn't want to go.'

'I think, particularly after this, she could be persuaded. It means you putting your foot down, though.'

'Oh dear. I don't want to.' Sarah didn't look at Tom, but at Gethin. 'It's all so difficult for me.'

'Sarah,' interrupted Tom. 'Don't turn to Gethin for sympathy. I've told him about the charade up at the hospital.'

Sarah blushed and stammered as she spoke. 'I panicked. I'm sorry. Oh, don't hate me, Gethin. I didn't want to lose Tom, but I couldn't let Lizzy down either. I didn't know what to do.' She burst into noisy tears.

Holly glanced over at Gethin, but his lips were tight and his hands clenched. It was Tom who turned to Sarah. 'You know I've forgiven you, Sarah, but you have to stop all this. I need to take this job. We'll be much better off and be able to help Lizzy through university, which you do know she needs to go to. The course there will be better for her as well. You have to be a good mother, show her the right way.'

Sarah had stopped crying. She bit her lip. 'But–'

'Seriously, Sarah. I put up with a lot, and I don't mind because I love you, but you always take Lizzy's side. This once I need you to stand by me. Lizzy is upstairs. This needs sorting out now.'

Sarah sniffed. 'I'll go and speak to her. I'll do what you ask.' With that, she made her exit up the stairs. Holly heard her go into Lizzy's room. Everyone breathed a sigh of relief.

'I think I'll go and join in the tete à tete upstairs,' Tom said sternly, and left them.

Gethin put his head to one side. 'Fancy a walk, just you and me? Not climbing mountains; we're not equipped for that, but just out here in the woodland.'

'Yes.' Holly felt the warmth of excitement for the first time since they arrived. 'Shall we take a picnic?'

'In this?'

'Mm...'

He laughed. 'OK. Come on, then.'

They packed up bread, cheese, paté, chocolate, mince pies and a thermos of coffee. They left a note for the others and left.

It had stopped snowing. Everything was very still. Here was the calm and tranquillity they both craved. In the distance they could see thick snow-covered mountain tops, set against a grey sky waiting to send more snow. They entered the woods. The ground was hard and icy, the leaves frozen shapes, the branches of the ancient giant oaks bowed with snow instead of leaves.

'Do you know, Snowdonia was the first National Park? It covers eight hundred and twenty three square miles. Nearly twenty per cent of it is woodland. They call it the Celtic rain forest.'

'Have you been on the internet before we came?'

'It was in the booklet in the cottage,' said Gethin, smiling.

'I love it in here,' said Holly. 'These oaks are hundreds of years old. Think of all they have seen here. It puts all our problems into perspective, doesn't it?'

As they walked, the snow silenced their words. Soon they came to a crystal-still river.

'Picnic time,' said Holly.

They found a log and sat on it, opening the food. A robin sat in front of them singing for crumbs.

'If I wasn't frightened of dying of frostbite, I'd like to stay here with you for ever,' said Gethin.

Holly poured the steaming hot coffee into cups. 'It's wonderful, magical.'

Her face burned with cold and the warmth of the sun reflected on the snow.

'You are so beautiful,' said Gethin. 'There are so many things I don't tell you often enough.'

'We have a week left here.'

'That's not long enough. I just love being with you,' said Gethin. 'You know, my happiest times are always with you. Even doing every day things like the shopping. I want to be with you.'

'I feel like that.'

'Do you?'

'Yes. Didn't you know that?'

'I always hoped.'

'Well, it's true.'

Gethin leant over and kissed her. He looked deep into her eyes. 'I love you so much. You know, I'd want to say that to you every day for the rest of my life.'

Suddenly, even the robin went silent.

'And I want to hear it every day for the rest of my life,' whispered Holly.

Slowly, the cold crept into their coats. They made their way back to the cottage.

As soon as they were inside Lizzy approached Gethin.

'Dad, Kane and I have split up.'

'Ah–'

'It's OK. You don't have to pretend to be sad.'

'What happened?'

'Mum and Tom talked to me. Mum said I didn't have a choice: I had to go, and then Tom told me about the course up there, and it does sound good. So, anyway I spoke to Kane–'

'And–'

'Dad, he went mad. I was scared. He shouted at me, said if I loved him I'd choose him over Mum, over courses, everything. He admitted to sending the texts. I said he'd upset Holly and he went crazy again.'

Gethin put his arm around her. 'It's not fair what he was asking you. You have your whole life ahead of you.'

'I want to go to university.'

'I know, and you should.'

'I did talk to some of my friends. Turns out they didn't like him much, said he was a bit creepy.'

'Sounds like you might be better off without him.'

'Mum said that.'

'Did she now?'

'Mm.'

'Good.'

That evening, to Holly's surprise, Sarah and Tom offered to clear up the evening meal and so she, Gethin and Lizzy went out and made a snowman by moonlight. The moon glistened on the snow. The trees were silhouetted against the sky.

Afterwards they went in for hot chocolate, listened to carols and rested in the dark with the lights on the tree. The clock struck twelve.

'Hey, can we pull some of the crackers? You know, those posh ones you put on the tree, Lizzy,' said Holly.

'Why not,' said Lizzy.

Holly reached up, and handed out the crackers.

'Now, I have to say that these are more aimed at the female members of the group. We do outnumber you men, after all.'

They sat in a circle, crossed hands and pulled them. Even Lizzy was impressed with the gifts inside.

'Wow, no tiny packets of playing cards that no-one ever plays with, or nail clippers that don't work,' she said.

'Look at these.' She held up a pair of silver leaf drop earrings.

Tom had a silver compact which he swopped with Sarah for the cufflinks in her cracker. Holly was admiring a silver fountain pen when Gethin came over to her. In the palm of his hand he held a silver ring.

'Want to swop?' he asked quietly.

'A ring?' she said.

'Would you like to wear it on your left hand?'

Holly smiled, tears glistened in her eyes. She let Gethin slip the ring on her ring finger. He smiled. 'We'll get another one soon–'

'No, this is just right. In fact, this is a perfect Christmas.'

Give and Take

'You're over-reacting. No-one got hurt, did they?'

Nathan's words were like a sharp finger poking and prodding my brain. I pushed open the door, my head thumping from lack of sleep. On the desk Jessica, the owner of the salon, had put a beautiful vase of daffodils. It was May 1st. My dream spring wedding was in five days' time.

I glanced in the giant mirror and scowled at my reflection. I looked a mess. In my job looks matter. Looking like this puts off the clients and maybe, despite making another appointment, they would just not return. It didn't take a lot, even with long term clients: get sloppy or over-familiar, and the client can be lost. No matter how often you've squeezed them in for a special occasion, politely excused them when they forgot an appointment, in a snip of your scissors they've gone. I cared about my job and my reputation. I wouldn't allow a row with my fiancé ruin that.

I rushed past the other staff into the cloakroom, pulled out my makeup bag, and put on a second layer of everything. Then I pulled out some of the grips holding my hair up, brushed it vigorously, then, using a pile of clips and bands, put it back up. It was a severe updo, and gave me a headache, but Nathan liked it. I guessed it also kept it out of the way for work. I imagined the veil I was going to wear on top of it. I had always had a picture of flowers threaded though my loose blond curls, but I knew Nathan would prefer this. Glancing in the mirror, I gave myself a quick smile of approval. The person looking back at me now at least looked the part of a senior hairstylist. My job involved me acting calm and friendly. Whatever might be happening, the show must go on. I pushed open the door, and walked on to the stage.

'Alright my luver?' said Jessica in her thick Bristol accent. 'Enjoyed your hen on Saturday. Bit tame, but suppose it's good for me not to get totally blattered for once.'

'I'm glad you enjoyed it.'

'Your Nathan back from Prague then?'

'Last night.'

'I saw some of the pictures online. They certainly know how to have a piss up,' Jessica said, laughing.

I swallowed hard. 'It seems so.'

'Still, it's harmless. Lads will be lads.'

I cringed at the words. Then I heard the door of the salon open and saw Peter, my first client of the day, come in. I wasn't the only one to notice him. Every head, male or female, turned subtly in his direction. Tall, good looking, wearing Calvin Klein white jeans, tight striped T shirt and Armani shades, Peter was my most glamorous client. The only thing that annoyed me about his looks was that he insisted on keeping his hair too long at the back: apparently Michelle said it made him look classy. It didn't: it aged him, looked scruffy, and completely clashed with the rest of him.

Peter and his wife, Michelle, have been coming to me for about ten years now. They make an interesting couple. Both about fifty; in contrast to Peter, Michelle is cuddly, homely, dreamy, and wore layers of cotton and silk, her hair shoulder length, brown and curly. She looked the part of an owner of a small craft shop in Clifton here in Bristol. She stayed wonderfully unimpressed by her husband's life as a fashion photographer.

I watched Peter walking towards me. Like a good therapist, or a doctor, it was second nature for me quickly to sum up my client. Nathan thinks I exaggerate my role, but he doesn't understand. I get to know people in a way others may not. My clients tell me things they might not tell anyone else. Today I noticed, like last time, there were subtle changes in Peter. He didn't make immediate eye contact; there was no easy smile.

'Hi Peter,' I said, holding out the nylon cape. He was much taller than me. I didn't attempt to put the cape on him, but let him do it himself. We walked to the chair. I noticed him lay a paper bag down, which obviously contained a book, next to the products and some magazines.

He sat down. We talked to each other through the medium of the mirror.

'What is it today?'

He took off his shades and, as dull brown eyes looked back at me, he said, 'Oh, I think the same as before. Don't you?'

'Of course. Maybe a bit off the back?'

'Better not,' he answered. This had become a standing joke between us. It usually raised a smile, but not today.

To try and lighten the mood, I said, 'You reading then?'

'Friend at work lent it to me, said it would do me good.' He turned red, but obviously didn't want to talk about it.

'Right, let's wash your hair first then.'

We went over to the basin. I liked to wash my clients' hair myself, even though Jessica said it was not good practice for a senior stylist. However, most of my clients were people I'd known for years. To be honest, I think they expected it.

'So how are the family?' I asked, shouting slightly over the hand-held shower.

'The children are fine. I'm away a lot at the moment. You know, with this magazine work up in Manchester.' That is where he and Michelle had lived before moving here. I had always had the impression that the move here had been some kind of fresh start for them and, from the odd remark here and there, understood that Peter had been involved with someone else up there.

Peter had been looking up at the ceiling, but suddenly twisted his head back to look at me. 'How did you find Michelle last time you saw her?' The water accidentally sprayed in his eyes. I wiped his face, not sure what to say.

'What did you think?' Peter repeated.

'She seemed pretty, well, maybe a bit….excited?' I said, as vaguely as I could. Actually, I thought she had seemed very on edge, laughed too loud. Her eyes had been darting around. Normally a good listener, she missed a lot of what I said to her. It wasn't like her. I turned off the shower, and wrapped Peter's head up in a towel. We returned to the seat.

As I combed through his hair, I noticed his hands were tightly clenched on his lap.

'Michelle was telling me about extending the shop,' I said.

'Yes, the café.' I saw his fingers dig into the back of his hands.

'So, there'll be an artisan bakery as well?'

'That's right.'

'How exciting.'

'You think so?'

Hearing the resentment in his voice, I glanced up from Peter's hair. I saw the stony look on his face. He had always seemed so easy going, but he was obviously not happy about this. It seemed to me unfair. He had had complete freedom to develop his career. Michelle had been the one at home bringing up the children. Now the children had left home, it seemed reasonable that Michelle should want to find new things to do.

'She seems very excited about it all,' I said. 'I think it could go well. She was telling me you both knew the baker; he's into all this new artisan bread. It'll go down well around Clifton: plenty of people there who don't have to go to Lidl for their bread.'

Peter let out a long, deep audible breath. He caught my eye in the mirror. He glanced at the engagement ring that I wore on a special pendant to keep it away from all the products we use.

'So, how are your wedding plans going?'

'Oh, OK, thanks.'

'Less than a week now. You've not taken the week off?'

'No, it's all organised. I'm just taking Friday off.'

'Michelle showed me the pictures from Nathan's stag do on Facebook. One of her customers is a friend of his. Enjoying his last nights of freedom they say, don't they?'

I cringed inside but smiled.

'I hope it works out for you, anyway,' said Peter, but there was no smile.

'Thank you. I do know marriage takes work. Everyone keeps telling me that. Plenty of give and take, they say.'

Peter gave a rather lopsided grin, then put his head to one side, which was rather annoying, as I had to stop cutting his hair. ''You give, she takes.' That's the saying, isn't it?'

I held the scissors very still and our eyes met in the mirror. His eyes were not smiling. 'That's a bit unfair. From what I see and hear in my job, it's usually the other way around.'

He shrugged, then said, 'So did you sort out that business with the wedding shoes?'

I smiled and went back to cutting his hair. Most men wouldn't have remembered that. I guess it made a difference, Peter being in fashion.

'Ah, yes. Sorry, I'd forgotten you got caught up in that.'

'Your Mum rang in the middle of my appointment.'

'I know. I wouldn't normally interrupt work for personal things.'

'So what happened in the end? Did you keep the shoes?'

'I did. Mum refused to take them back. I could have, but I gave in. Mum and Nathan think I should wear heels for the wedding. The trouble is, they are huge heels, which I never usually wear. Working here, standing all day: well, it would be impossible. I've tried wearing them around the house, but they are agony. Mum says I'm exaggerating, but I didn't exaggerate the blister.'

'So, what will you do?'

'I'll have to wear them now. The dress is the right length with them.'

'Doesn't seem fair. I mean, I see these girls wear those shoes for shoots, but you shouldn't be hurting on your wedding day.'

I stopped and froze. The words suddenly seemed to reach way beyond the sentence he had uttered.

'Are you alright, Lisa?'

'Sorry,' I said quickly.

'It's OK,' he said, but he looked puzzled.

At that moment, Jessica came over, carrying the appointments book.

'Lisa, Jane Palmer is on the phone. Like, you were meant to be doing her hair the day after tomorrow, but could you fit her in this afternoon?'

'She wants highlights?'

'Yes.'

I stifled an irritated sigh. 'Let me have a look.'

I glanced over at the diary. 'Peter, sorry. I'll be two minutes.' I added, 'It's not shoes; it's work.'

I scanned the diary. 'Tell her if she comes in at half three I can start her colour off. Then I've got some dry cuts, kids after school, then her...Yes, I could manage it. Thank you.' I wasn't going to admit in front of a client that I would now have to work late, but it was frustrating.

However, the interruption had given me time to catch my breath. 'So, how are the children doing?' I asked.

Peter immediately started telling me their news. He might be away a lot, but his children are everything to him.

He talked on about the children as I finished the cut. I held up a mirror behind his head. 'OK?'

'Fine,' he said, but he wasn't looking.

As he left, he said, 'Oh, good luck on Saturday. Hope you have a really special day. Ignore old cynics like me. Have a great day.'

'Thank you.'

As I watched him leave, Jessica came over to join me.

'Well, what's got into George Clooney, then?'

'What do you mean?' I asked.

'He's lost his sparkle. Maybe Michelle is trying to lay the law down.'

'He seemed rather bitter.'

'She might have given him an ultimatum. You know, 'You have to choose between her or me.' Still, she won't push it. Bet she can't believe her luck: landing a bloke who looks like that and managing to hold on to him all these years.'

Suddenly, I felt so annoyed: had some women not moved forward at all?

'Michelle is a lovely, bright woman. Without her he wouldn't have great kids and a beautiful house to come home to. In any case, marriage is about being equally respectful of and caring for each other.'

43

Jessica laughed. 'You've a lot to learn. There's always an underdog, and it's usually the woman.'

Before I could reply, Jessica grinned annoyingly and walked off.

When I arrived at the salon two days later, I noticed that Jessica had brought in a new bunch of flowers. The daffodils had not lasted long. Today it was peonies. I wondered if I had told her they were the flowers that I was using in my bouquet: I was having light pinks and whites; the same as my bridesmaids.

I touched the petals gently: silky smooth and soft. It would be so easy to crush them, destroy them. Last night I had tried to re-write my wedding vows. The words I had written before somehow sounded hollow, empty. I'd asked Nathan if he had written his.

'Oh, yes. I downloaded some,' he had replied.

'You haven't written them yourself?'

'Shit, no. Wouldn't know what to say.'

I had looked away, and he had tutted, irritated. 'It's only words. Don't get so uptight.'

'Only words....' Does putting the word 'only' in front of things miraculously diminish them? 'It's only money.' 'Only sex.' If you could do that all the time, how were you to know what was important?

I glanced at my appointments for the day, and saw that Michelle was due in first thing. I looked forward to seeing her. She was a survivor. It would be good for me.

Michelle arrived promptly. I was pleased that she had lost the edginess that was there last time, but she hadn't returned to her old calm self. Her step was purposeful. She walked straight towards me holding out her light jacket.

'Morning, Lisa.'

'Hi, Michelle.'

I followed her to the chair, and put the cape on her.

'So, how are you?' I asked her through the mirror.

44

'I'm very well.' She threw the words out defiantly.

'Good,' I said, relieved but rather intimidated. 'So, usual?'

She pursed her lips. 'No. I want a change.'

'Tell me what you'd like done.'

I started to comb through the tangled mass of brown curls. Her hair, parted in the centre, hung like a curtain with her face peering out. It was a dull brown with some grey, but lovely and thick. It had been like this all the time I had known her, apart from when she had had it dyed about six months ago: a slightly darker brown, but that had grown out now.

'I want it short, like a bob, with a fringe.'

I looked up, surprised. 'How short?'

'Up off my shoulders. It's how I used to have it years ago.' She gestured with her hands.

'Wow. Maybe we should do it a bit shorter today, and see how you find it?'

'No. I know exactly how I want it, and I want it coloured.'

'Today?'

'Have you got time?'

I nodded. 'Actually, I have. Someone cancelled.'

'Good.'

'Right. Well, I think we'll do some of the cut first. Then we need to talk colours. Let's go and wash it.'

Michelle came over to the basins and I wrapped towels around her shoulders. As I washed her hair, I said, 'You've always liked your hair long, haven't you?'

'I've only had it like that since coming here. I never liked it though.'

I thought of all the times she had said how pleased she was with her hair. It goes to show you never know for certain what people are thinking.

'So how are all the plans?' asked Michelle. I breathed out heavily.

45

'Everything alright?'

I blinked, and looked at Michelle in the mirror. 'Yes, of course. Just a bit stressy.'

'Good practice for married life.'

I glanced up, but she wasn't laughing. She looked cold. Then she said, 'I'm surprised you're working this week.'

'Oh, people have things on, need their hair doing. I have to come in.'

I busied myself cutting Michelle's hair, then we looked at the chart of strands of hair to choose colours, picking out a combination of warm browns.

I applied the colour, and asked, 'So how are the plans for the café going?'

'Really well. My premises have been massively under used. You know, I used to be in catering in Manchester. I'm really looking forward to that side of it. It's very exciting.'

I smiled, genuinely pleased that she had something new in her life, and thought of Peter's mean spirited words about her working late.

I finally washed off the excess colour, finished the cutting, and blow dried Michelle's hair. When I had finished I was shocked at the difference.

'You were right,' I said. 'You look very different.'

'Thank you so much,' Michelle said. She touched her hair nervously. 'That feels like the real me.' She smiled at herself confidently. She stood up. 'Enjoy Saturday, and remember the key to a good marriage is give and take.'

'So people keep telling me.'

She smiled again. 'You'll be alright: plenty of give in you.'

When she had left, Jessica said, 'Michelle looked amazing.'

'Thanks. It looked good, but somehow she didn't look like Michelle.'

'I guess it's part of the game of keeping her man: lay the law down and then make him glad he stayed.'

I screwed up my eyes tight. 'Why does it all have to be a game, Jessica?'

Her eyebrows shot up. 'It's the way it is.'

I walked over to the window and watched Michelle walking down the high street. So she had won this time, kept her man: won by giving in. 'Plenty of give in you,' she had said to me. So would that be me one day? I knew then that I had to talk to Nathan.

The next day I went into work very early. I hadn't slept all night. I felt numb with tiredness and spent emotion. I would have to ring Mum soon; she was going to go mad. I looked at the peonies: drooping now. I blinked away tears. To keep myself busy, I started robotically sorting out the towels, until I heard someone knocking on the glass door. To my surprise, it was Peter. He looked awful. Unshaven, but not in a trendy way. He had pulled a coat over his clothes. Maybe it had been harder this time, giving up the other woman. I didn't feel sorry for him, though. Michelle deserved more.

'Hi, Peter–'

'I left my book,' he said, his voice flat. 'My friend wants it back.'

'Oh, right. Hang on.' I went over and found the book had been pushed among the magazines. As I handed it to him, I noticed my hands were shaking.

'Are you alright?' he asked.

I nodded, forcing a smile to stop me crying, but it hurt.

My lips were trembling. I couldn't speak.

He put down the book and put his hands gently on my shoulders. 'What's happened?'

'You won't understand.'

'Understand what?'

47

'It's different for women.'

'What is, Lisa?'

I took my phone out of my pocket and found the pictures. Glancing down, they still shocked me. They were taken at Nathan's stag do. These were the ones not put on Facebook. I handed the phone to Peter. 'Bet you think these are funny, don't you?'

He scrolled though the pictures of Nathan in a lap dancing club; the girl dancing, on him, then the two of them walking away together. Nathan turning back winking and making an obscene gesture to his mates. I watched his face closely, waiting for him to laugh. However, he looked very serious.

'It might not be what it looks like,' he said, eventually.

'It is. Although the pictures were sent by a friend, Nathan didn't try to pretend nothing had happened. In fact, he told me he'd slept with another girl later that night. Seemed quite proud of it.' I looked straight at Peter. 'He says it doesn't mean anything, that no-one got hurt. He said that for our relationship to work there had to be give and take. But, you know, it really hurts. I can't pretend it doesn't, act like it never happened.' I turned on Peter angrily. 'You men think you can do anything as long as you come home, but it hurts; hurts because you wanted someone else. It's about respect, trust. And then, to tell us we're not hurting: that just makes it worse. Don't tell me what I am and am not allowed to feel.'

Peter blinked. 'I've never heard you like this, Lisa. You sound very angry.'

'I'm sorry. I forgot you're a client–'

'We've known each other a long time. What's the matter? You're getting married in two days' time: you should be so excited and happy.'

My hand automatically went to where my pendant had been. 'I gave Nathan the ring back last night. I'm not getting married.' The words spoken out loud startled even me.

'My God. Why not?'

I glanced down at my phone. 'I expect you think I'm mad. Everyone else will. I'm dreading telling Mum.'

Peter shook his head. 'No. I don't think you're mad. You have every right to be upset that Nathan slept with those women.'

'Really?'

'Of course. I'm the last person to play down what you're feeling. Nathan has betrayed you, and he's broken your heart. To tell you then you aren't hurting: that's so cruel.'

I didn't understand. If he knew how much he had hurt Michelle, why had he done it?

'You look confused. What is it?'

'Nothing.'

'Tell me.'

'Well, you seem to understand, but you cheated on Michelle, didn't you? Don't you feel guilty?'

To my amazement he laughed a loud, ugly laugh. 'You think that?'

'Yes. It's why you moved here, isn't it?'

'We moved because Michelle had an affair in Manchester.'

'Oh, no.'

'Yes. The move was meant to be a fresh start, but you see we never talked about it properly. Or when we did, she said it was nothing, just a physical thing. She said I had to learn to give and take. She never said sorry for hurting me; didn't think she had. She never saw she'd done anything wrong.'

'I never realised.'

'Men and woman are both capable of treating people badly.'

'Yes. I guess so. Still you've forgiven her, and you're still together.'

'Actually, we're not. Yesterday I finally told Michelle I was leaving her.'

'Oh no.'

'It's OK. It's been on the cards for a while now. We've been having long talks. It's why I asked you how she was last time I saw you. I was actually worried about how she would cope if we split up.'

'Really?'

'Yes. You see, although it has always been her that has seen other people, she has also always told me she needs me; that I am her rock. I believed her.'

'So what happened since then? It's only been a few days.'

'To be honest, the hair cut was the final straw.'

'What?'

'You see, it's how she has it done for him. She should have known how much it hurt me to have that done.'

'I don't understand–'

'When we came here, it was to get away from the man she was seeing. She used to have her hair short for him, even though I liked it long. When we came here she grew it out. It seemed symbolic of her giving him up.'

'But why has she had the cut now?'

'Because she has invited him here, to Bristol. He's a chef and is going to work in this new venture with her.'

'Oh no.'

'Yes. I was horrified when she first told me he was coming. She said I was over-reacting: it was over with him. He's only a work colleague now. And, you know, I tried to believe her. Then she started working late, didn't come home one night. 'It's only sex,' she said, and, 'I always come back to you. You have to learn to give and take.' Peter spat the words out. 'I'm so tired Lisa, tired of trying to make something work, trying to pretend things don't hurt. Do you know the play, Educating Rita?'

'I saw the film: Julie Walters and Michael Caine. I remember the woman was a hairdresser.'

'That's it. Well, for me, one of the most moving parts is when Rita's mother looks around at them all singing in the pub and says something like, 'There has to be a better song to sing than this.' Well, it's how I feel now. I'm tired of the old, flat song of my marriage. There has to be something better.'

My heart beat faster.

'Yes. That's it. That's how I feel.'

It was like meeting someone else who shared some hidden, secret, illness: finally someone who understood.

Peter laid his hand on mine. 'I know it seems like you are in hell but, believe me, it's better to find out now. You need and deserve someone who loves you, respects you, who is loyal to you, who never ever wants to hurt you.'

I looked at myself in the mirror, and started to take all the pins and bands out of my hair. I could feel my forehead relax. I shook my hair out, feeling free.

'I guess I won't have to spend a day in heels on Saturday,' I said, and tried to smile.

'You look very pretty with your hair down,' said Peter.

'Thank you. It's a relief to wear it in the way I like, but Nathan said it looked better up.'

'Nathan was wrong.'

The words sounded daring, but Peter was right.

'Yes. He was wrong about a lot of things.'

'Thank you. You know, I always think of myself being the one to help my clients, but today you've really helped me.'

Suddenly, I smiled a proper smile. I could feel it reach up and light up my eyes. It seemed a long time since

I'd smiled like that. Peter looked confused. 'What are you thinking?' he asked.

'You know, Michelle was wrong about a lot of things as well.'

'I know.'

'I don't mean just things in your relationship, either.'

'What else, then?'

'It was you mentioning Educating Rita: remember what happens near the end?'

'Frank goes away?'

'Before that. Rita says something like, 'I'm going to take years off you.''

Peter still looked confused. I laughed.

'All I'm asking is: please, let me cut the back of your hair properly for once. I could do it now.'

Peter grinned. 'Yes. You know, I realise now I never liked it. Thank you.'

I grinned back. 'You look out for me. I look out for you: give and take.'

The Key

Ruth was petrified. She stood alone on the concourse of Gatwick railway station. She was waiting where she was told, outside Smiths, next to the Train Information Desk, but she was sure that at any minute he might find her; she was still trapped in the nightmare.

When she had woken that morning she had assumed it would be like any other day. Then she had heard the doorbell ring. She was puzzled: it was too early for the postman. Ruth had got out of bed, put on her dressing gown, and answered the door. She had been surprised to find a courier with a letter which had to be signed for. It had been sent express the day before from Toronto, Canada. The courier told her that it must have cost the sender at least fifty pounds. Ruth guessed that he was curious, but she simply signed and took the letter. Recognising the writing, Ruth knew who the letter was from, but was astonished that her daughter Kim should spend that kind of money just on a letter. Whatever was wrong? They had hardly communicated for weeks now. First, Ruth's laptop had crashed. Then she had lost her mobile and, even when she talked to Kim on the landline, they kept losing connection. Ruth was anxious for news. She was about to open the letter, when her husband Harry came into the hallway. 'Who was that at the door?'

'A letter from Kim at last. Express, though. Whatever can it be about? She's paid a small fortune to send it this way. I know she's fed up of all her letters getting lost in the post, but this must be something important.'

Harry took the letter from her. 'That's great; we'll save it for after breakfast.'

'But–' Ruth really wanted to read the letter.

'I got up early especially to make you the pancakes you asked for last night; please don't let them go cold. Come on, all news is better after hot pancakes.'

Ruth frowned. She didn't remember anything about pancakes, but she could see he had made an effort; the letter would have to wait. Then she noticed Harry glance at an empty hook on the wall.

'Sorry. I was sure I put them there yesterday,' she said quickly.

'It's alright. We'll find your house keys later. Don't worry.' Harry gave her that sad smile which she was getting used to.

'You're so patient with me.'

'You're not to worry. You know what the doctor said. Now, I've laid the table,' Harry said, 'You go on in. I'll bring the pancakes through.' He headed for the kitchen while she went to sit at the table in the living room.

The table was set: guest perfect.

'Can I pass you the cafetiere?' Harry called though the hatch. 'I managed to track down that coffee you liked: the one you said was perfect for breakfast.'

Ruth went to the hatch, but was confused: she always drank tea for breakfast, didn't she?

'You prefer coffee now,' said Harry gently, as he handed her the coffee.

'Oh, thank you.'

Did she? Did she really prefer coffee now? How long had she been doing that?

Ruth sat down and looked out of the window. There was a lovely early morning haze promising another hot day. The garden looked pristine. Harry worked so hard out there; even the grass around the pedestal for the stone bird bath was perfect. She would never tell him, but sometimes

54

she missed the disorganised chaos of her garden back in Stoke. There, she had created a cottage garden, a riot of tall daisies, columbine, delphinium, giant hollyhocks, and lavender, with their heady scent. It had been her slice of paradise in the city but, of course, that sort of garden would never suit Harry. He liked order: neat trimmed borders, straight paths, and now, of course, his roses, which stood to attention in regimented straight lines. This was his domain.

She watched as a sparrow flapped in the stone bird bath, the sun catching the droplets of water bouncing from the surface. In the distance, a strip of sea shimmered. Harry was right: Worthing was a lovely place to live.

'Here we are.' Harry's voice startled Ruth: she hadn't heard him come into the room. He gave her a plate of pancakes, each neatly sugared and rolled; quarters of lemon neatly arranged at the side.

'Thank you,' she said. People were right: he was one in a million.

Four years ago, Ruth's life had been derailed by the sudden death of her husband, Dave. There had been no warning. He had left for work in the police force as usual one morning, and never come back. His death had not been on the streets: it had been in the station. He had got up to make a coffee, collapsed, and died from a heart attack. It had been that sudden.

Ruth had been left paralysed by grief. Dave and she had planned their future so carefully. In three years he would have retired. They had saved hard, and were going to buy a motor home to travel through Europe. Her daughter Kim and husband John had discussed their plans to emigrate to Toronto in Canada. Although initially Ruth had been horrified, Dave had encouraged it. He said that as a doctor and a lawyer they would have a good life. One day he and Ruth would go and join them. It had all been planned. But then Dave had died, and all the plans they had made had been torn into tiny pieces and thrown to the wind.

Ruth had gone into a kind of living coma, moving robotically from room to room, meal to meal, day to day. Then she had met Harry. She was still working part time in the library. She remembered the first time he came in. He looked like a retired army officer, standing very tall, with a head of silvery hair, but he also looked rather lost.

'Can I help you?' she had asked.

He had blinked. 'I want to research sixteenth and seventeenth century cabinet making.'

Ruth had liked the earnest way he spoke.

'We have some books. Also, you can use the computer if you would like.'

'I prefer a real book.'

'So do I,' she had said.

He had smiled. 'I'm Harry; good to meet you.'

Ruth found herself drawn into his research. It was like it awakened a curiosity, and in turn gave her life some purpose again. The reason for Harry's interest was that he was a retired cabinet maker who had been making bespoke furniture in Manchester. Now he had retired he wanted to give himself a really challenging project to use the time he had on his hands. His dream was make a replica of an Italian eighteenth century secretarie and chest: one with many secret drawers and compartments, a work which involved as much engineering as craftsmanship.

One day she met Harry for coffee. They were sitting outside, as she was smoking at that time. She noticed that he looked preoccupied.

'Is something wrong? Can I help?' she asked.

'My divorce came through today.'

Ruth had been surprised. Whereas she told him a lot about her own circumstances, he said little about his.

'I'm so sorry. I assumed you were widowed like me.'

'No. It was my second marriage, actually. She's had a good lawyer, definitely getting the better part of things financially.'

'Oh dear–'

'It's not easy, is it? Managing on your own.'

'No, but I'm fortunate. Dave had provided for me with good insurance, and I have a lump sum from his police pension for a rainy day. So, did you have children?'

'Not with my second wife, but with my first wife I had a daughter.'

'Ah.'

'I don't see her, though. My first divorce was a bitter one. She was a difficult woman who turned everyone, including my daughter, against me.'

'Oh, that's awful. I can't imagine not seeing Kim.'

'Well, we were never that close, to be honest. It's the way it goes. Anyway, I moved here from Manchester to make a new start. I have to say, I like the way things are going.'

He touched Ruth's hand, and smiled shyly.

'By the way, you don't need those, do you? I mean, it's very bad for you, and I want you to live for a very long time.'

He looked at the cigarette in her hand.

'I started again after losing Dave. You're right: I ought to give up.'

'Well, no time like the present,' he had said, laughing. 'Come on: hand them over.'

Ruth had stubbed out the cigarette, and handed Harry the packet from her bag.

'The lighter?'

She bit her lip. The little gold lighter was a present from Dave but, still, if she kept it, maybe she would always feel like a smoker.

'OK.'

He had put them in his pocket. 'Well done.'

Harry turned out to be kind and charming; all her friends liked him. The only person who had a problem with him was her daughter, Kim. Initially, Harry found her rather overwhelming.

'She must frighten the life out of her patients,' he said. 'Still, I expect they all behave for her.'

'She's a very good doctor, actually. She has always been very close to both of us. She's been our life, you see,' said Ruth.

'So she doesn't want to share you,' replied Harry.

'I think that's it,' she said, grateful that he was being so understanding.

Ruth tried to find ways for them to meet and get to know each other, but it was Harry who suggested building some cupboards for Kim's bathroom. To Ruth's embarrassment, Kim had asked 'But how do I know you are any good?'

Ruth saw Harry blush, but then he had taken out a newspaper cutting from his wallet and handed it to her.

Ruth saw Kim's eyebrows shoot up. She handed the cutting to Ruth.

"Manchester cabinet maker, Harry Price, who works for bespoke furniture makers, Bostons', has been commissioned to make a bespoke cabinet for the newly refurbished study in Windsor Castle." With the article was a photograph of Harry standing in front of a stunning piece of furniture.

'Harry, I never knew–'

'I don't usually tell people,' he had said, and quickly put the cutting away before looking at Kim. 'I hope you will trust me to make your bathroom cupboard.'

'Of course,' mumbled Kim. Even she had had to admit that he did a beautiful job.

'I put in extra effort,' said Harry. 'I really want us to get on as a family.'

Ruth had been seeing Harry for almost a year when he asked her to marry him. She said yes immediately, but she had been nervous about telling Kim.

'I don't know, Mum. It's so quick.'

'It's been nearly a year. You like him now, don't you?'

Kim had shrugged. 'It's a big move. You'll lose your independence.'

'I never wanted that. I like having the company.'

'He makes a lot of decisions for you.'

'I like that as well. He's a sensible, intelligent man.'

'He's very charming,' Kim conceded.

'Well then–'

'I can't put my finger on it–'

'You'll get used to him: you'll see. He's different to Dad.'

'Dad was so open. You always knew what he was thinking. I'm never sure with Harry.'

'He's a bit more careful, that's all. Your Dad could be rather blunt, you know.'

'It's not long now till John and I go to Canada. You will still come, won't you?'

Ruth had seen the root of Kim's problem. She knew that Kim dreaded living so far away from her.

'Of course we'll still come. I've talked to Harry about it. But we don't want to come straight away. See how you and John settle first. I know you both have good jobs out there, but I don't want to have all the upheaval of selling my lovely house and leaving my friends, to find you wanting to come back within a few years. I've seen it happen to people who've moved to be by their children and then been left high and dry in some back of beyond place.'

'We know what we're doing.'

'Good. Now, you should be pleased I won't be on my own while you're out there settling in. We'll come and visit soon.'

'But why not wait a while to get married?'

'I don't want to. I hate living on my own, and the idea of another winter coming home to a dark empty house fills me with dread. No, if we get married soon, you and John will be at the wedding. To be honest, you're the only ones that matter to me.'

'Does Harry have a large family?'

Ruth shook her head. 'Not really. It's so sad. He's a good man. I hope soon you'll come to like him.'

'Whose house will you live in?'

'Oh, mine. His is small. He had to give his ex a lot on their divorce.'

The wedding was very quiet, just as Ruth had wanted. She wore a smart light blue outfit. Harry wore a navy suit. Afterwards they went to a hotel in the heart of the Peak District not far from where they had lived.

It was soon after this that Kim and John emigrated to Canada. The move affected Ruth more than she expected. There was only five hours time difference, but with Kim working it meant that the casual chats they used to have seemed to change. The four of them would sit down and Skype together once a week. It was nice that Harry wanted to be involved, but she missed the private chats she and Kim used to have. It was the same with emails. Harry would always see them first, although she was the one to answer. Kim sometimes sent her texts, but the long letters she said she sent never seemed to arrive. Ruth found herself counting the days until they could go out and visit Kim and John.

However, Harry had surprised her one day by saying, 'You know what? Me and you should move to the coast, go somewhere new. Start afresh.'

'Oh no. I couldn't–'

'Why not?'

'I dread leaving here but, when I do, I thought it would be to move to Canada.'

'That's not going to be for a few years, is it?'

'Well–'

'No. We must be sensible. Let's make sure they are going to stay there first. It doesn't mean we can't make a visit, though.'

'What were you thinking?'

Ruth was soon to find out. The following day, a beautiful sunny day in June, Harry had driven her to Worthing. They walked along the front, looked out to sea, and walked along the pier. It was enchanting.

'I've never lived by the sea,' said Ruth. 'The air is wonderful.'

'You see, we could have a good life here. You know, until we move out to be with Kim.'

Ruth smiled. 'And we have the lump sum to use. The house would be an investment.'

'Exactly'

'It's wonderful here. Yes. I think you're right.'

Her house in Stoke sold quickly. They found the perfect bungalow, not far from the seafront, with room to display all Harry's wonderful pieces of furniture, including the secretaire he had completed.

Initially all went well. Ruth had been thrilled to see the way Harry thrived. He soon started a new project, making them a swing seat for the garden. However, he had also branched out into new interests, in particular growing roses. He had recently been elected chair of the parish council. Like his roses, he had flourished. Ruth was content to enjoy her new home, and took to walking along the seafront.

They had been in the bungalow eight months when Kim and John had come back to spend Christmas in the UK. The visit had gone well, although Ruth felt Kim was rather critical of Harry.

'He's a bit bossy, isn't he, Mum? Likes everything done in a certain way–'

'Like you,' laughed Ruth. 'Seriously, I don't mind, and he does so much for me.'

'He's the one going out making friends, though.'

'I'm fine. Harry is far more sociable than me.'

'But you don't seem to be as independent as you used to be. Are you going to try and get work in the library here?'

'Maybe. I'm very happy settling into my new home, you know.' Ruth could see that Kim didn't understand. At the end of the day, she was getting older. Maybe Kim didn't like it.

One day during the visit they all decided to drive to Eastbourne along the coast.

'Are you going to drive, Mum?' Kim had asked.

Ruth had been surprised. 'Harry usually drives nowadays.'

'Well, you don't want to lose your confidence, Mum.'

'I suppose not.'

'Kim's right,' Harry had interrupted. 'Ruth, you drive us today.'

'Well, alright. I'll get my keys.'

Ruth had reached up to the hook Harry had put up for her keys, but they weren't there.

'Oh, Harry. Do you know where I put them?'

He had laughed. 'Oh dear, not again. Hang on. I'll check the bedroom.'

He had come back holding the keys aloft. 'There we are.'

'Thanks, love. I don't know what I'd do without you.'

It was on Christmas morning that Kim had shared the wonderful news that she was pregnant. She and John had shown Ruth and Harry photos of their lovely home and were keener than ever for them to move out and join them. Ruth had been enthusiastic: the thought of her first grandchild drew her like some irresistible force. She felt she had to be there, to see her grandchild growing up.

As soon as Kim and John had got into the taxi to the airport she had asked Harry about going for a visit in the summer.

'Of course. It would be lovely to go,' said Harry. 'But I think we should wait a while.'

'But I want to see the baby as soon after he or she is born as I can.'

When Ruth had seen the look of surprise on Harry's face, she had realised again how different it would have been if she had still had Dave. He would have been so thrilled at the idea of a grandchild. He would have been booking tickets then and there, probably for weeks before the baby was due, just to make sure. Still, it was bound to be different for Harry.

'The thing is, August and September are prime months for all the garden shows, and I really stand a chance with my roses this year,' he had said.

Ruth had frowned. 'It's very difficult.'

'You do see I can't go, not this year,' Harry had said. 'Anyway, I expect Kim and John would like some time to adjust. It's a big thing bringing a baby into your lives.'

Ruth understood, but she knew that she was desperate to go. 'Listen, why don't I go on my own, just for a month? It would save money just paying for me, and you wouldn't have to miss your shows.'

'You don't want me to come with you?' Harry had looked hurt.

'Of course it would be nicer to travel with you, but this is a good compromise. I am happy to order tickets well in advance. I can save a lot that way. The baby is due August the third so, if I book a flight for the first of September, it's bound to have come and Kim will be ready to see me then.'

Harry had stroked her hair and smiled. 'As long as you don't mind me not coming, I think that would be a very good idea. I just want you to be happy.'

The next time they skyped Ruth had told Kim.

'That's fantastic, Mum.'

'It will just be me. Harry has his shows and things.'

'That's great, and how are you, Mum? How are you keeping?'

Ruth was surprised. 'I'm fine, love. Why are you asking?'

She saw her daughter hesitate.

'Is something the matter?' Ruth asked.

She saw Kim look across at Harry then back at her.

'The morning we left the UK, Harry told me he was worried about your health.'

Ruth was shocked. 'Whatever for?'

'He said you were getting forgetful. Didn't you, Harry?'

'Well, yes,' he had mumbled.

'That's nonsense,' said Ruth. 'I don't forget things any more than my friends. You know, the usual 'Where are my reading glasses?' type of thing.'

'I was surprised when he said it. You seemed fine when I saw you.'

'I am. Honestly, love. He's just being over-protective.'

'Good. Mum, you're a bright independent woman. Don't forget it. I shall send you some leaflets that I give to people about how to keep your mind active. You look out for some work at the library. When I was over I saw that they were asking for volunteers on the mobile library. You'd be great at that. Be good for you.'

'I'll think about it, and I shall read the leaflets you send me, well, if they actually arrive. The post is terrible,' Ruth said. 'Now, tell me how you are feeling.'

When she had finished the call, Ruth said to Harry, 'What's this you've been saying about me getting forgetful?'

He had blushed. 'I didn't like to say anything to you.'

'I don't forget things any more than other people my age. You're not to worry.'

'Well–'

'What do you mean?'

'It's little things: forgetting the mince pies in the oven, leaving your bag in the restaurant.'

'Oh, that's nothing.'

'Do you know at the moment where your house keys and mobile are?'

'Not exactly, but I could find them.'

'Of course. Listen, take no notice of me.'

Ruth had tried to forget the conversation, but it niggled at her. Was she forgetting things more?

The following week she had lost her purse. She had no idea where it was. She picked up her handbag to go out, noticed it was light, and found it was missing. They had searched the bungalow but it was never found. It was a nuisance as all her cards had to be changed. The following week, when exactly the same thing happened again, she started to worry. She realised she was losing things on a daily basis. Sometimes they never found them. She had had two sets of new keys cut.

Harry remained patient and kind, but she was worried. She went to the doctor, who seemed unsure of what was going on. He talked to her about stress and gave her medication.

Then, in March, things took a more serious turn. Harry came into the living room one morning looking very concerned.

'What's the matter? What have I done now?' she had asked.

'I've just had a phone call from our credit card provider.'

'What's happened?'

'They wanted to check about a large amount being paid out.'

'Oh no. Has the card been stolen?'

Harry shook his head, then showed her his laptop.

It showed an acknowledgment of an order on Amazon made by her for garden furniture costing two thousand pounds.

'But I never ordered that.'

'You did, love. I've been through the order. Remember, you asked me if you could use my laptop?'

'Well, mine had crashed again.'

'Yes, I don't mind that. You said you were looking at garden furniture.'

'Yes, but that was for a new parasol, nothing like this. How ever did I do that? I must have clicked something by mistake.'

Harry shook his head. 'There are lots of safeguards. Don't you remember anything?'

Ruth shook her head.

He had looked very serious. 'This isn't the first thing, you know.'

'What do you mean?'

'I cancelled a loan you applied for the other day: five thousand pounds. The rate of interest was astronomical.'

'Oh, God. What's happening?'

'I don't know, love, but we could end up bankrupt if we're not careful. If you don't mind, I'll change the passwords. Then, whenever you want to order things, we can do it together. Is that alright?'

Ruth had nodded miserably. It was all so humiliating. When she next skyped with Kim she couldn't bear to tell her.

However, the following week, something even more serious occurred.

Harry had gone out to a meeting which involved being out for lunch and an evening meal. Before he left he said, 'Could I ask you a big favour?'

Ruth had smiled; it was gratifying that he still felt he could ask her to do something for him.

'Of course. What is it?'

'Could you take this cutting around to someone from the committee? I've written the name and address down. It's a fair drive, take about half an hour. Will you be alright?'

'Of course. I know where that is.'

'Thanks, love. I said you'd be there at two. She'll make sure she's in. Also, if she asks you in for a cuppa, would you mind chatting? She gets lonely.'

'Of course not. No, I'd like to.'

Ruth had eaten her lunch and then, according to her, she went out at about half past one. The drive took her half an hour. She stayed with the woman from the committee for a cup of tea. It was just gone three o'clock when she returned. However, it was to find a fire engine outside the bungalow. The front door was open. She ran in, to find Harry looking shaken.

'What's happened?'

'It's the kitchen: there's been a fire.'

'But how?'

Ruth could see that he didn't want to tell her.

'You're not to worry.'

'What happened?' she repeated.

'The fireman said it was started by a lit cigarette in the waste bin. They even found the charred packet on the side.'

'That's impossible.'

'It's the brand you used to smoke.'

'I haven't smoked since that day out with you, a couple of years back now. I gave you the packet, remember, and the lighter.'

'I noticed two packets in your side drawer the other day. One was nearly empty. I didn't like to say anything. Anyway, it was lucky. I got bored in the meeting and decided to come back early.'

'But I couldn't have done this. I don't have any cigarettes in my room. Come and see.' Ruth had dragged Harry into their bedroom and pulled open the drawer. To her horror, she saw a new packet of cigarettes.

'I don't understand.' she said. 'They couldn't be the ones you took off me, could they?' she said, knowing how ridiculous that sounded.

He shook his head. 'No. I definitely threw away the packet and the lighter. You see, the lighter's not there, is it?'

She shook her head miserably and burst into tears.

'Oh Harry. I'm so sorry. What's happening to me?' She gave him the packet. 'Please, get rid of them. I never want to see them again.'

'Of course. Listen, the main thing is that no one was hurt. It's mainly smoke damage in the kitchen. It was lucky the hatch was closed. We'll be able to put it right.'

Ruth went back to the doctor. This time she was referred to a clinical psychologist.

When they were Skyping she tried to talk to Kim.

'It all seems very odd. You would remember smoking, surely? I know you'd given up.'

Ruth sighed. She could understand her daughter being in denial, but this had to be faced.

'You don't see me, love. If it wasn't for Harry I'd be in a right state. I could have burned down the house.'

She saw Kim look at Harry. 'It was lucky you came home early.'

'It was,' said Ruth quickly.

'Mum, I don't understand.'

'Love, you don't know everything.'

'Well, what else?'

Ruth was embarrassed: it was awful telling her daughter these things, but she told her about the money.

'So you can't access your bank account now, Mum?'

'Only with Harry: it's better that way.'

'Mum, you're still going to come out to see us, aren't you?'

'Of course. I have my ticket.'

'Good.' Kim looked at Harry. 'You make sure she does, or I'll be sending my lawyer husband over to fetch her.'

Ruth was embarrassed. 'Kim that's enough. Harry looks after me incredibly well. He's patient and kind. You should be thanking and supporting him. After all, you and John are not here, are you?'

Feeling very upset the conversation was over, Ruth was glad when Kim ended the call.

Ruth kept her appointment with the psychologist but the report seemed to take a very long time to arrive.

'I keep ringing his secretary, but she said he's very behind with his paperwork.' Harry tried to make things easier for her. He placed a small table in the living room for Ruth to keep her mobile, glasses and the remote on. He went with her to the cashpoint and the supermarket. It was so odd: she would go to pick up the kiwi fruit and he would say, 'Don't you remember? I'm very allergic to kiwi,' when Ruth had been sure she had put them in the fruit salad the week before. The cereals she never got right any more. 'I always have porridge / granola / weetabix:' she could never remember which.

One morning Ruth went into the bedroom and took out the ticket to Canada: she was starting to dread the thought of going.

Kim's baby was born on time. They received a very excited phone call from John at three in the morning: it was a baby boy. They had called him David after Kim's father. Ruth felt very emotional. The distance between her and Kim had never seemed greater, but she was worried about the journey.

One morning, Harry said gently, 'I've been thinking about your trip to Kim and John.' For one moment, her heart leapt: maybe he was going to come with her, but then he said, 'Are you sure you still feel up to it?'

She sighed. 'I want to see them.'

'Of course, but when you think of that journey—' Harry started to go through all that was entailed until, eventually, Ruth said, 'You're right. I know it. I can't do it, can I?'

'I'm so sorry, love. If you find me the ticket I'll see what I can do about a refund and, don't worry, in the New Year we'll go together.'

'That report still hasn't come through?'

'Sorry, still not come.'

Ruth bit her lip.

'I found that leaflet on your desk the other day,' she said.

'What was that?'

'About a lasting power of attorney.'

'Oh no, I never meant for you to see that.' He looked shocked.

'It's OK. I'm glad I did. I think it would be a good idea if I gave that to you.'

'No. No way,' said Harry.

'Yes, love. It has to be. I want to do it now while I can think straight. I thought I would talk to John about it, you know, him being a lawyer.'

Harry sighed. 'Good idea. Although I have a friend on the gardening committee; he's a lawyer who specialises in these things. It might be better to have someone impartial talk to us and arrange it.'

'You could be right.'

'And I think it's best not to say anything to Kim yet. Let's have a chat with him first.'

As Ruth had sat nibbling at her pancake this morning she glanced out of the window at the garden. The sparrow had flown now.

Harry looked up from his pancake.

'My friend, remember, the one from the committee who is a solicitor, is coming this afternoon.'

'Of course.'

'You are sure now?'

'Yes. It's the right thing to do.'

'As long as you're sure. By the way, you haven't given me the airline ticket yet. I need to contact them.'

'Of course. I'll look for it later.'

'Oh, and did you record the snooker for me last night?'

Harry took a bite out of a large apple.

'Sorry. Did you ask me to?'

'It doesn't matter. It's not important.' Ruth could see that Harry was trying to hide his irritation. He stood up, stretched, and embraced the day. 'I'm off to shower.'

Harry started to walk to the door, but stopped. He walked over to the secretaire which he had made. Ruth assumed he was looking for something. However, Harry didn't open it at that moment. Ruth realised he was looking down at the small wooden table next to it, the designated place for her to keep her mobile and other things. He stood there staring.

'What's wrong?' she asked.

'Still not found your mobile?'

Ruth glanced at the table, miserably.

71

'Never mind. Maybe you could go and get the airline ticket for me, then make me a shopping list. I'll go into the supermarket after my meeting this morning and, when I come home, I'll sort out the ticket.'

Glad to escape, Ruth hurried into the bedroom. She opened the drawer to her bedside cabinet. The second drawer down was where she kept important papers. She opened it now but looked in horror: the ticket wasn't there, and for that matter neither was her passport. What had she done with them? She heard Harry getting into the shower, and decided that she would go and make the shopping list; she could have a good look for the ticket when he had gone out.

She started to make the list. It was while she was trying to remember what kind of milk Harry liked that she thought she heard a noise in the living room. Thinking that maybe the neighbours' cat, a frequent visitor, had come in, she went to the hatch. But it wasn't the cat: it was Harry in his dressing gown. Ruth was about to ask him what he was looking for when something in his manner stopped her. He was slightly hunched up, and seemed to be creeping and looking around suspiciously. It was very odd. Maybe he was trying to cover up for some mistake she had made. She watched, but realised that she could still hear the shower running. Ruth pulled back so that she could peep through the crack. She saw Harry take a small cufflink box out of his pocket and, from that, the piece of felt from the bottom. From under that he took a small key, with which he opened the secretarie. Ruth found herself feeling quite detached. It was interesting. She had always wondered where he kept the key but, as she knew it was his private desk, had never bothered to ask. He pulled out the box-shaped pigeon hole. Carefully, he lifted the base. Ruth could see a secret compartment. She watched Harry now taking something out of the pocket of his dressing gown. She peered more carefully, her sense of detachment now gone. Even from where she stood she recognised her house keys: the key ring had a maple leaf on it which Kim had given her at Christmas. Harry placed the keys into the compartment, then replaced the pigeon hole. Why on earth was he doing that? However, he then moved on to a similar compartment on the other side of the desk. From it he took a phone: she recognised the sparkly pink case she had bought for it. But why was Harry hiding it in there? Harry was looking at it intently. He switched it on, seemed to go through her texts, then switched it off and replaced it. Finally, she saw him take out of his pocket the letter she had received from Kim that morning and put it in the compartment with the phone. Quietly, he replaced everything, and locked the secretaire.

Ruth frowned, completely baffled. What was going on? Maybe it was his way of keeping her things safe? However, what happened next she found deeply disturbing. Harry picked up their wedding photograph. He turned sideways, so that she saw him smile. However, it wasn't a loving smile. The malevolent look on his face shocked her and, for the first time, she felt frightened of him. She had seen that smile years ago on the face of a girl as she had slowly pulled the wings from a live butterfly. Harry put the photograph down and left the room.

Ruth swallowed hard. She blinked. Was she imagining this? She didn't trust herself anymore; maybe she was just going mad. She heard the shower switched off and Harry return to the bedroom to dress. Quickly, she finished the list as he came into the kitchen smiling.

'OK, love. I'll be back in about two hours. You rest this morning.'

Ruth looked at him, feeling very confused. He seemed so normal; had she just imagined all that had happened?

'You OK?'

She nodded.

'Good.'

'I'll have a go at sorting out the flight ticket when I get back. You know where you put it, don't you?'

Again, Ruth nodded.

'Good.' Harry kissed her on the top of her head. She watched him walking down the hallway, smartly dressed in a light summer jacket and blue trousers: he was always immaculately dressed. She watched him leave the house, took a deep breath, and looked out of the window, seeing him drive his car away. She desperately wanted to read that letter from Kim, but she knew that Harry would be furious if she looked in the secretaire. She checked out of the window again: he'd gone. He would never have to know, would he?

Ruth rushed into the bedroom and rifled in his drawers until she found the cufflink box. She found the tiny key, and made her way down the hallway. She checked again that Harry's car was still not there, and entered the living room. Nervously, she opened the secretaire. She found the letter easily and put it in her pocket. She then found her phone, and her keys. Standing looking at them, she tried to understand again why Harry had put them there. Why make her think she had lost them? He knew how much she worried. He could have said that he had put them safe but wasn't going to tell her where. She switched on her phone. She was shocked to see that everything had been deleted: all her messages, address book; everything was gone. That was what Harry had been doing, but why? She remembered that there were more secret compartments. She closed her eyes and tried to remember the plans. Yes, pull this one out. Then she saw them: her ticket and passport. She gasped. How odd. She kept looking. In another drawer she found the lighter Dave had given her. Harry had told her he had thrown it away. Beside it was the packet of cigarettes. Again, what was that doing there?

Ruth thought back to the fire. An idea started to creep into her mind. It was odd that she didn't remember anything about smoking. Was it something more than good luck which had brought Harry back early to the bungalow? Thinking about it, it had been odd that he had asked her to go out on that errand.

She shook herself: this was madness. She kept looking. She found the purses she was meant to have lost, but what she found next was probably the most shocking of all. Tucked at the back were a pile of letters, all opened, all but one from Kim. As she glanced through them she saw that some were dated from months ago. There was no reason for Harry to be hiding these from her. Among the letters she found the report from the psychologist. Again, she wondered why Harry had hidden it. Did it say things that were so upsetting he thought it was better she didn't see it? She sat down and read it. It appeared that the psychologist was confused by Ruth. She had done well in all the tests and, apart from Ruth appearing stressed and anxious, he did not feel able to make any kind of firm diagnosis at this time. He suggested the GP monitor her condition and contact him if he had any further concerns. So, really he was saying that she wasn't ill.

How odd: why had she been losing everything, then? She opened the latest letter from Kim, which had arrived that day, and which was still sealed.

Dear Mum

I hope you get to read this. I am very worried about you. I know you think that you are unwell, but I am sure you're not. Please believe me. I don't want to write this, but I am very concerned that Harry is trying to make you think you are ill. You remember that film we saw, that black and white one with Ingrid Bergman? It was called Gaslight. The husband tried to make his wife think she was going mad by making the gas lights flicker when he'd told her he was out.'

Ruth sat back and frowned. She remembered the film; she had found it very disturbing. Was it possible that Harry was doing this to her? She read on.

I have always been worried about Harry but, when you told me about the money, I became very concerned. I remembered that cutting he showed me and where he had worked in Manchester. I decided to look a bit more into his background and, Mum, I hate to say this, but something is very wrong. I rang the firm and was very lucky to be put through to a very chatty and indiscreet secretary. She told me that Harry had left very suddenly. Apparently, he told everyone that his wife had left him for someone younger, but someone else there knew her. What had really happened was that she'd become really frightened of him. He was very manipulative. She'd thought she was going mad until friends had made her see what was going on. Word got around and then, without warning, Harry left. Someone heard he'd moved to Stoke. Mum, I really believe he is a very dangerous man.

John is coming over. He is getting a flight to Gatwick this afternoon and should arrive tomorrow. If you manage to see this letter, go to Gatwick to meet him. Otherwise he will come to you. I know this all seems very dramatic, but I am very worried. Please trust me on this. Don't say anything to Harry.'

Ruth sat, staggered by what she had read. She heard a noise, and turned round. She was very scared. She didn't want to believe Kim, but she knew deep down that what she said was true. Strangely, though, it wasn't all the things that she had just found that convinced her. It was remembering that look she had seen on Harry's face when he had smiled in that awful way at their photograph. That was when she had realised that he was a dangerous man.

Quickly, she got dressed. She grabbed her phone, her purses, the air ticket, and her passport, and dashed out to her car. She drove to the station, all the time looking around, convinced that Harry would know what she was doing. Fortunately, the next train to Gatwick via Hove was arriving soon. Ruth caught it, but still felt on edge. She kept looking around for Harry. She took out her phone, and sent a text to Kim, who answered quickly: John had arrived and was heading to the station; she would text him. Kim told Ruth that when she arrived at Gatwick she should wait at the railway concourse, by WHSmith, and John would find her.

That is how Ruth came to be standing alone at Gatwick, feeling frightened, lost and alone. She heard a voice call her name and saw a man in a light coloured jacket coming towards her through the crowd of people. The light shone on his hair, making it look almost white. It was Harry. Ruth started to shake, her breathing shallow and hard. He had found her. Her head started to swim. Ruth closed her eyes tight, and grabbed pointlessly at the wall behind her.

'Ruth, are you alright?' The voice sounded a long way away.

'Ruth, it's alright. It's John.'

Slowly, she opened her eyes, then she started to cry. Through the sobs, she said, 'I've been so scared. Am I really safe now?'

John held her close. 'Yes, Ruth. You are. The nightmare is over.'

The Right Shoes

Emma looked up the beach to the esplanade and saw the graffiti covered, boarded up shops, the scruffy amusement arcades and run down hotels. This was Ruxton on a typical cold, drizzly, late September Sunday morning. She could feel her feet getting wet, the pebbles digging into her Gucci loafers. The shoes had been a present last Christmas from her mother and may have suited the streets of London but not the beach at Ruxton. Her mother knew how unsuitable the shoes were but maybe they had been her way of carrying on her protest at their move. She had never wanted Emma and Chris to give up their well paid jobs in London to go to Theological College, but when, as they approached the end of their studies, they told her they were going to be working in the deprived seaside town of Ruxton she was furious.

'You're throwing your lives away,' she had said. 'You can't do this to Flora. You can't take her to a place like Ruxton. She may be only six but my granddaughter is a bright child who needs stretching. You've already taken her away from a fantastic school in London; left behind excellent ballet, singing and violin teachers.'

The arguments continued right up until the last term of college. Then something so unexpected and devastating happened that all arguments were silenced. A sudden, brutal death in the family had torn up any talk of the future and left Emma and her mother paralysed. Emma, as a young child, had lost her father after a long illness, but nothing prepared her for this. She had somehow seen out her final days in college but it was as if she was watching a ghost acting her part.

The cold salty breeze hit Emma's face. She looked around, and tried to remember how she had felt when they had arrived in Ruxton a year ago. All her remembrances were shrouded in a deep nagging sadness. She hadn't allowed Chris to tell the congregation what had happened to her just before their arrival: she couldn't bear talking about it to strangers. Flora had been miserable for months after coming here and her tears had substituted for Emma's unshed ones.

However, as Emma watched Flora this morning rummaging among the pebbles she realised that her daughter had undergone something of a transformation since the summer holidays.

'Come and look at this stone,' shouted Flora from across the beach.

Emma started to make the painful walk over stones towards her daughter. Flora's blonde hair had escaped from the tortoiseshell slide and it flew around, as wild and as untamed as the sea. Flora grinned, her cheeks burning red with excitement. 'This is fossilised wood,' she said.

Emma took the stone and ran her fingers over the raised black areas on it. 'Are you sure?'

'Yes. I learned about it in school. You know, there were dinosaurs down here a long time ago; both herbivores, the one who eat plants, and carnivores, the ones who eat meat. They've found fossils of footprints on the beach, mainly adult Iguanodons; those were plant eaters.' Flora took a deep congratulatory breath at the end of the difficult sentence.

'Gosh, you know a lot about them.'

'Miss Price has been telling us. I wish they were still here. Could you imagine a Tyrannosaurus Rex charging along the beach?'

'I think I'd be rather scared.'

'Oh, Mum. Don't be such a wimp. It would be exciting.'

Emma smiled. It was wonderful to see her daughter laughing again. Flora had spent her last school year hiding in an invisible shell. However, after a relaxing summer holiday spending hours on the beach, and now having an enthusiastic new teacher, the old Flora was re-emerging. Emma watched as Flora intently drew a picture of her find in her diary, brushing her fair hair out of the way with the back of her hand. She was struck again how much she looked like Lizzy.

Wonderful, beautiful Lizzy had been Emma's older sister, and their parents had adored her. They all had. Lizzy was kind, funny, clever. After university she had eventually become a barrister and lived in a gorgeous house in Hampstead. It was Lizzy who had taken Emma's mother to Covent Garden, to tea at the Ritz and to the Queen's Garden Party. And then, as impossible, scandalous even, as it seemed, it had been on Lizzy that the tragedy had fallen. Their precious girl had been killed. It was as if somebody had gone into the National Museum and set fire to Picasso's Girl with a Dove. Lizzy's death fifteen months ago had seemed the pointless destruction of irreplaceable beauty.

Flora's likeness to Lizzy, which had always been striking, became precious. Watching Flora miserable here had been heart breaking. It led Emma to think her mother had been right and that they had made a terrible mistake coming here.

Flora called to Emma again. 'See this on the rock: these are small fish bones, and that shiny circular black bit is a tooth belonging to lepi something. I'll have to ask in school again. I've forgotten the name.'

'We could go to the library. When we move to Surrey they have a huge library we can go to.'

Flora's mouth had pursed tightly, a gesture that reminded Emma of Lizzy.

'We are still going then?' asked Flora.

Emma sighed. 'Yes, of course.'

'But why? We've only just come.'

'Because when Dad was offered the new job you were very unhappy here; you were saying the dancing and violin lessons here were boring, and you hated school. You said you had no friends, the work was too easy, and we had tears every day.'

'I didn't cry.'

'You did, love. It's why we started coming down to the beach before school, to cheer you up.'

Flora looked around. 'Maybe I was a bit sad, but coming here in the summer and having Miss Price as my teacher has made it alright.'

Emma screwed her face up in frustration. 'Look, we had to say 'yes' to this job before the summer. It's a unique job. Dad will be perfect for it and, as I said, we were really thinking of you.'

Flora, however, wasn't listening. 'Miss Price really likes my diary. You know, she did a degree in, hang on, it sounds like planets but it was about fossils and things.'

'Do you mean palaeontology?'

'That's it.'

'That's impressive.'

'She knows everything there is to know about fossils, and this place is full of them. It's wonderful.'

Despite her irritation, Emma smiled. Flora didn't see the dilapidated buildings. All she saw was a whole world to discover.

'We'll still be able to go to a beach on weekends,' Emma said gently.

'But not here. Not every day.'

'You'll have great new teachers in your new school and there will be new things for you to do. It'll be like when we lived in London. There'll be proper singing lessons in the school; the uniform is much more grown up.'

'I'm very comfy in my sweatshirt and trousers.'

'You'll be going horse riding. Someone in the church has offered to give you lessons at reduced rates.'

'So we won't be paying the same as the other girls?'

'No. Even on more money, we couldn't afford that.'

Emma saw Flora scowl, and tried a different tack. 'It's also a great opportunity for Dad.'

'You say that, but he doesn't smile when he talks about it.'

Emma didn't reply. Flora was right, of course. To leave here so soon after arriving had been a very difficult decision for Chris. He had been contacted by the church they had attended in their working days up in London. That had been a very large, affluent church which had three morning services to cater to the size of the congregation. They wanted him to go and lead a mission church in Surrey they had opened. He would be provided with a refurbished beautiful old house; the local school was fantastic; and the pay extremely generous by church standards. Flora would have access to all those things she had had in London. Chris had been reluctant but Emma, worn down by the tears from her daughter, was sure it was the right place for them.

Emma looked down at Flora. 'Just think, we'll be able to afford proper holidays; no more camping in the rain.'

'I like camping. We could come here. I've seen a campsite.'

Emma's eyed widened, but she didn't comment. Instead she said, 'And we promised you could have your own mobile when we get there.'

'What about a dog?'

Emma screwed up her eyes, and looked at Flora. She had obviously saved her ace till last. 'I know you want a dog. Every child wants a dog.'

'When we move, can we have a dog?' persisted Flora.

'One day.'

'Mind you, a dog would like the beach—'

Emma gritted her teeth. Gosh, Flora was like Lizzy, verbally twisting and turning. Lizzy had always won the arguments.

'If and when we get a dog we can take it to a beach sometimes. And in the new house we will have a huge garden for it.'

They heard church bells in the distance.

'We ought to go,' said Emma. 'Daddy will wonder where we are.'

They clambered up the beach. Emma looked down at the sea: the tide was on its way out, and soon there would be a stretch of sand. She had to admit that even she had grown to appreciate coming to the beach. She loved the sound of the waves shushing over the pebbles, the fact that each time they came here it was different.

'We had someone come into school to start a choir,' said Flora.

'Really?'

'Yes. He used to sing in big operas. Miss Price said we're very lucky. He's coming in for free.'

'That's great.'

'I had to sing for him to be allowed to join the choir.'

'You never said. How did you get on?'

'Oh, I got in. He said I had a good voice.'

'Gosh. That's great.'

'Skyler got in as well.'

'Ah.'

Skyler came to the church with a woman called Debby. Although Skyler called Debby 'Mum,' Emma wondered if she was adopted. Debby was quite a bit older than the other mothers and Skyler looked very different to her.

Emma's relationship with Debby was difficult and had got off to a bad start. On the second Sunday after their arrival, Emma had turned up with what she had described as 'some decent coffee and homemade cakes' for after the church service. Debby, who always went to the cash and carry for the coffee and biscuits, was offended. Emma remembered the chill that had passed around the church hall. People had sipped the coffee and nibbled on the cakes, but the following week they returned to cheap coffee and basic biscuits. Emma felt firmly boxed in by Debby, and probably a large portion of the congregation, as the posh woman who didn't fit in.

In her state of numb grief it had suited Emma to hide away, and keep her involvement to a minimum. As a trained teacher, however, she had offered to work with the children and had even been prepared to run the groups, but Debby was already in charge and had resisted letting her take over. It was very frustrating as, despite being very popular with the parents, Debby was not that good with the children, tending to be loud and bossy, making the children in turn difficult to manage. Emma tried to hint at ways of improving things, but Debby was easily offended and became defensive; there seemed no way forward.

Emma and Flora drove up through the town, out to the new estate. She parked their car in front of their small estate house which came with the job of minister. From there, they walked to the church. The estate was a mass of new brick flats and houses, with neat white doors, concrete paths and tiny gardens. Most of it was social housing. There were none of the parks, restaurants, theatres and shops of Surrey: just street after street of houses. Everywhere there should have been trees and grass there were cars, parked bumper to bumper. The front gardens grew yet more cars on concrete driveways instead of flowers.

They reached 'The Well', a large, new, rectangular building, which to Emma's mind looked more like a gym than a church. She saw the people all heading down the path. Her stomach clenched as she saw Debby.

'Morning, Emma,' shouted Debby.

Emma plastered on a smile.

'Have you remembered you are on coffee?' Debby asked.

Emma gritted her teeth: of course she had.

'I've put a nice new jar in the kitchen.' Their eyes locked.

'So, Flora, are you going to come out to your group today?' asked Debby.

Emma reached down and held Flora's hand. 'Flora can decide.'

'OK. Skyler was asking, that's all,' said Debby. Skyler, a little dark-haired elfin child, stood confidently beside Debby and smiled over at Flora.

Emma and Flora went into the church. Chris came over and looked anxiously at them. 'Morning,' he greeted them. Emma hadn't seen him yet that morning. He had been off early to Morning Prayer.

'Hi, love,' she said. 'We've been down the beach. Haven't we, Flora?'

Flora held up her fossil. 'I found it.'

Chris looked at it carefully. Emma knew how busy he was, but he never rushed Flora.

'It's wonderful. Did you draw it in your diary?'

'Yes. I'm going to show it to Miss Price.'

'That's great. See you later.'

When it came for the children to go out to their groups, Emma saw Flora watching the children. 'It's OK,' she whispered. 'You can stay with me.'

'No. I want to go out, Mum,' said Flora, and left her.

It was a quiet, thoughtful service. In London, they had had a highly accomplished band and slick, projected services. You never simply sat: even in the prayers you would have puzzles to put together or music playing. Here, Chris would guide the congregation through familiar prayers, and they sang a few hymns accompanied by the piano. There was always a time of complete quiet and stillness which Emma appreciated. In these quiet moments she had time to think, to remember Lizzy, to miss her.

Emma watched Chris, and was aware that he had changed. He had expanded with the work, matured. He had worked so hard to gain the trust of the people here. With a pang of guilt, she knew he would miss it, but then he would be taking on a lot of new responsibilities, and it was the right thing to do for Flora. Also, if she was honest, she felt it was the right thing for her. Coming here was tangled up with losing Lizzy. She felt she had made a mess of things; she needed a fresh start.

After three quarters of an hour, Emma saw the children return. Flora returned trailing a soggy picture with pieces of coloured maize and glitter falling off it. Emma frowned. She saw Debby looking over at her and tried to smile but, honestly, why couldn't Debby do something more interesting? The children always did the same things with her.

Emma went out into the kitchen to put the kettles on. In the hall, through the hatch, she could see Debby busy tidying up, but they didn't speak. Emma put the value biscuits on the plates and spooned discount coffee into thick white china cups.

People came in and were greeted by Debby. Emma served them coffee. Afterwards, as she cleared up, she was surprised to find Flora had left her side. She could see her talking to Debby in the hall. When Emma went to fetch her, Flora came running up to her shouting, 'Mummy, can we have one?'

Emma blinked, non-plussed. 'Pardon? Have what?'

'A puppy. It's Skyler's Mum: her dog has had puppies, and Skyler says we can have one.'

Emma frowned. She certainly didn't want to get bamboozled into getting a puppy on spec like this.

Debby came over. 'Skyler had no right to offer Flora a puppy. Sorry.'

'Please, Mum. She said we could have one,' pleaded Flora.

'No, I don't think so,' responded Emma.

Debby looked down at Flora. 'Having a puppy is a lot of work and responsibility. You don't just get one on a whim. They have to go to a good home that wants them.'

Emma felt offended at the implication that her home was not good enough for one of Debby's puppies.

'I'm sure we could offer a very good home to a puppy,' Emma said stiffly. 'It's just that this is not the right time.'

'That's fine; it's not something you do lightly,' said Debby.

'But Mum–' said Flora.

Emma smiled coldly at Debby, and quickly left with Flora.

Flora, however, didn't give up that easily. When her father came home for Sunday lunch she started again.

'Is it such a bad idea?' Chris asked Emma.

'You know we will be moving soon,' said Emma, annoyed with Chris.

'But you said there would be parks and things–' interrupted Flora.

'I know, but–'

'So there isn't a problem,' said Flora, staring at her mother.

Chris grinned. 'She has a point.'

'Look, I'm the one who will have to look after it.'

'But Mum, you said you wanted a dog one day.'

'I know, it's–'

'So why not now?'

Emma sighed. 'I think, Flora, you should go and play, while I talk to Dad.'

Flora scowled at her. 'I think you should at least go and look at them.'

'I said you can get down now,' said Emma firmly.

Flora got down from her seat and stomped out of the room.

'It's all the wrong time,' Emma said to Chris.

'I don't see why. In fact, it might help Flora with the move. She's been asking for a long time.'

'I know,' Emma conceded, 'but to get one from Debby!'

'You know, Debby's alright. She's scared of you, that's all.'

'Nonsense. She can't stand me, thinks I'm some stuck up woman who doesn't understand anyone down here.'

'You should give her a chance. You can be a bit–'

Emma glared at him. 'A bit what?'

'Listen, we are used to mixing with people who are naturally very confident, people who have been given a lot in life, people like us. You know, to get anyone here to do something as simple as a reading is really hard, not because they can't do it, but they are so worried about getting it wrong, making mistakes. Debby is like that and she naturally finds you, a fully qualified teacher, a threat.'

'To be honest, I'm the one feeling threatened. Everyone likes her.'

'They like you as well.'

Emma shrugged and changed the subject.

'I need to check out the uniform Flora will need when we move. Maybe there will be a second hand shop, although Mum said–'

'We're not having hand outs from your mother,' said Chris sternly.

'Well, it will have to be a second hand shop then,' said Emma crossly. 'You know, down here I got her whole uniform for the cost of the school tie up there.'

'Everything will be expensive. It's crazy. Down here, I'm aware of earning more than most of the congregation. In Surrey, we will earn a lot less. Somehow, we just have to be ourselves, but it's not easy.' Chris fiddled with his knife and fork, arranging them on the plate. Then he coughed, and looked up 'Anyway, what about this puppy?'

'I don't know. Maybe I should go and look just to keep Flora happy. I could say it's the beginning of the search or something. I'm sure I'm the last person Debby wants to buy one of her puppies. The puppies will be a real odd lot, probably a mixture of half the dogs on the estate.'

'Listen, I'm going round to Debby's in the morning. We want to tie harvest in with the food bank. Why not come with me? You can have a look at the puppies. No commitment. We won't tell Flora yet.'

Emma reluctantly agreed.

The next morning, she accompanied Chris to Debby's house. She seldom went to the houses of members of the congregation. Nobody asked her, and she didn't like to invite herself.

Debby's front garden was very neat, with tidy rows of Michaelmas Daisies in the borders. As they rang the bell, Emma peeped through the window. On a thick pilled carpet of rather dark maroon stood a wonky wood-veneer table. There was a variety of chairs and sofas, all facing a large television screen. On the walls were photographs in cardboard frames of Skyler at various ages in school uniform. Along one wall was a long illuminated fish tank. Emma thought of her own minimalist room, with oak flooring and white furniture. The rooms couldn't be more different.

Debby answered the door.

'Emma has come with me to see the puppies,' said Chris. 'Hope that's OK.'

'Come on in.'

They followed Debby down a dark hallway into a large back kitchen. Here was a similar jumble of mismatched furniture and a washing machine that was noisily spinning clothes. In front of it sat the next wash, piled in a plastic laundry basket.

At one end an area was cordoned off in a pen containing three quite large puppies: one golden, two golden and white.

Their area was immaculate. The puppies were cocker spaniels. The mother, asleep in a pristine bed, was a beautiful golden colour. Emma followed Debby over.

'Don't let Flora nag you into something. You'll be the one walking out in the rain and carrying the poo bags.'

'I know. As Chris said, we've only come to look,' said Emma, irritated.

Debby leant over the wooden gate, picked up a gold and white puppy, and held it out to Emma. Nervously, Emma took the puppy.

'Is this right?' she asked, suddenly panicking. 'Am I holding him properly?'

'That's fine,' said Debby, who actually smiled at her. 'He looks very comfy with you. His name's Ollie. He's a cocker spaniel.'

Emma gritted her teeth. 'I realise that.'

'My Ruby is from one of the bitches we used to show.'

'Really?'

'Oh, yes. My Mum bred them. She taught me everything I know.' Debby glanced over at one of the many photos on the fridge, of a woman proudly standing in front of a black cocker spaniel with a rosette attached to her collar. Next to it, Emma spotted a photograph of a dark-

90

haired young girl, who looked very like Skyler. Debby followed her gaze and spoke quietly.

'That's, my sister.... Skyler's Mum.'

'Oh, I thought–'

'No. My sister was Skyler's Mum, but I've brought her up since she was a baby.'

Debby turned back to the puppies.

'Their Dad got to Crufts a few years ago.'

'Gosh. Really?'

'Yes. His owner is a friend I met at the shows. She offered her dog for me to mate with my Ruby. She thinks I should get back to doing shows. I always used to do them, but then I had Skyler to take care of. I'd like to start going go back to it now, take Skyler with me. Not Crufts: that's all too expensive, but maybe local places.'

'How exciting.'

Debby looked straight at Emma.

'So what are you thinking? You said you're just looking, but are you really thinking of getting a puppy?'

Emma looked over at Chris. He nodded encouragingly. 'We are serious.'

'You're leaving us after Christmas, though, aren't you?' Emma heard the accusation in Debby's voice.

'Yes, but we'll be surrounded by woods and parks. How many of the puppies have homes?'

'These are the only ones left. I'm keeping that little golden one. The two orange and white ones need homes, not that there is any rush. I've turned people down, you know. I'm very fussy. I usually try to visit, check out the home. Also, I like to know that someone will be around; cocker spaniels are not the sort you can leave for long.'

Emma held Ollie close, stroked the silky golden ears, then his tummy: it was warm and soft. 'He's a sweetie,' she said.

'Yes, the quietest one: always the last to get picked up.'

Chris started to stroke the puppy. He looked besotted. Emma glanced at him. 'What do you think?'

'I think if Debby is prepared to accept us, we would love to offer Ollie a home,' he said, decisively. 'We haven't asked you how much you charge for your puppies.'

Debby mentioned a sum. 'It's less than a lot ask, but it's the homes that matter to me. And, yes, I'd be happy for Ollie to come to you.'

Emma looked at Debby. 'I'd need time to get ready.'

'Of course. They've been ready to go for a couple of weeks now but, as I say, I'm in no rush.'

'Thank you,' said Emma, adding, 'It's all new to me, you see. This will be our first puppy.'

'I do classes in the hall every Tuesday. You should come.'

'You said you need to see our house, though–'

Debby shook her head. 'It's fine. I've been to a meeting there. Just check there are no holes in the fence around the garden, and you need to be prepared for accidents on the floor and chewed table legs.'

Flora, of course, was delighted. They decided to collect Ollie on Chris's day off, a Wednesday.

'Right: here is all the paperwork,' said Debby. 'You can trace his pedigree. All his checks have been done and he's had his course of immunisations, so he can be taken out to mix with other dogs.'

'Right,' said Emma; then she bit her lip. 'I'm very nervous, you know. I've bought all the stuff and read the books, but nothing prepares you for the actual puppy, does it?'

'You can always phone me,' said Debby seriously. 'In with the paperwork I've put some basic guidelines. There's so much out there on the web and things, but not all of it is good.'

'I was a bit horrified at some of the things I read, I must admit. It seems to me that rewarding the good things he does is better than punishing him. I guess it's my teacher training.'

'You are good with the kids,' conceded Debby.

The women stood looking at each other. Then Debby said, 'Anyway, when you come on Tuesday evening, you'll see all my training is positive. Don't you worry now: take time to enjoy him.'

Once they were home, Emma put Ollie on the kitchen floor and he urinated. Emma found the lead, put it on Ollie, and opened the back door. Ollie thought this was great fun and started jumping up at the lead. 'Come on, time for tiddles,' said Emma. Then she remembered that she was meant to give Ollie one of those treats. She rummaged in her bag and took him into the garden. Emma kept Ollie on the lead. She stood, saying 'tiddles' to Ollie, who ignored her and went around sniffing the grass. When he finally performed, Emma gave him a treat and they returned to the house.

Ollie ran around the kitchen, then suddenly dropped to the floor and lay very still. Emma rushed over in a panic, but realised Ollie had just gone to sleep, exhausted. Chris made them both a cup of coffee.

When Emma walked up to the school, she saw Debby with her group of mothers.

'How is Ollie?' Debby called out.

Emma usually stood on her own, assuming no-one wanted to talk to her. However, she walked over to Debby.

'He's OK. He's eaten a meal, been in the garden. He sleeps a lot, though. Is that alright?'

'Fine. They need sleep. It's a very exciting day for him: first day away from his Mum and family.'

'Of course.'

Another mother interrupted. 'Don't be too soft, though. Tonight, you just shut the door and let him howl; he'll soon settle.'

Emma had been reading about her first night with the puppy and said, 'Actually, I don't think I'll do that. I'll let him out if he needs to go to toilet, and I couldn't bear to hear him cry all night.'

Debby's eyebrows shot up, and she smiled. 'Well done. I've been working hard at toilet training. Ollie won't want to dirty his bed, so take him out if he needs it, whatever the time. It will pay in the long run.'

Emma smiled back at Debby. She felt she had passed some kind of test. Then she saw Flora coming out of school with Skyler.

'Mum, can Skyler come and see Ollie?' Flora asked.

Emma looked over at Debby, who nodded. Emma asked, 'Debby, would it be alright to bring Skyler back after tea, say, about half five?'

'OK, if you don't mind. You be a good girl now, Skyler.'

They went home. Emma watched as Skyler and Flora sat playing with Ollie. Skyler, used to puppies, was actually very good with Ollie. Emma found her really helpful. Skyler also enjoyed reading books with Flora, and they both sat giggling while doing some painting. When it came time for Skyler to leave, she said, 'Thank you very much for having me for tea.'

Emma replied, 'It was a pleasure,' and meant it.

That night, Emma took Ollie outside, then settled him in his crate. She had read the books, and made it as homely as she could, with soft blankets, a toy and water. She even left the radio on quietly, then went upstairs. She got into bed with Chris.

'So far, so good,' she said.

They read for a while, and turned off the light. Then the howling started. Emma went downstairs. She saw Ollie looking at her miserably.

'Come on. It's not so bad. I know you miss everyone, but we're your new family, and we love you very much.'

She let Ollie out of his pen, took him out into the garden, and settled him back down.

Emma was going back to sleep when the howling started again. She remembered Flora's tears before going to her new school. Change was so hard. She wanted to tell Ollie all the great things that they were going to do with him, all the extra fuss he would get, the toys, the complete devotion from Flora. But, of course, all he could think about was what he had left.

Emma went downstairs and opened the cage. Ollie ran out to her.

'Maybe just tonight–' Emma said.

She took the blanket out of the cage, carried Ollie upstairs and settled him next to the bed. With a sigh, Ollie flopped his head down on his paws and went to sleep.

The next morning, Chris laughed when he saw Ollie in their room.

'Well, that didn't take long.'

'You missed all the howling and, in any case, I took him out twice in the night.'

They went downstairs. Emma took Ollie into the garden. She was just getting things ready to go down to the beach before school, when Flora said, 'Mum, can we go to school a bit earlier? All my friends want to see Ollie.'

'Oh, OK. We could walk him to school then.'

For the first time, they set off to walk to school. Soon they were meeting other parents and children walking as well. Emma was pleased to see Flora chatting to the other children. All eyes were focussed on Ollie; Flora was enjoying the reflected glory. Emma had never found it so easy to talk to people here. Suddenly, she wasn't the

95

minister's wife: she was either Flora's Mum or, more significantly, Ollie's owner. Ollie loved all the fuss and stayed surprisingly calm.

The following Tuesday morning, Emma lingered in bed. The rain banged on the window, but that wasn't the reason she didn't want to get up. Today would have been Lizzy's thirty-fifth birthday. Even after they had left home Emma and Lizzy had always remembered each other's birthdays. They had a competition to see who could find the tackiest card. If it had 'to my super sister' on it, so much the better. They always sent each other a really good book. Emma for the past month had found herself occasionally looking at Amazon for a suitable one, then realising there was no longer any need.

Emma pushed back the duvet. Chris usually made sure he was around for this date, but the meeting he had already left for was very important

'I'm so sorry, love,' he explained. 'It is a crucial meeting. The Government are responding to that report about the needs of some of us neglected seaside towns and made grants available. However, we need to get in quickly before they get distracted and the money gets diverted to something else.' Emma had understood, and seen him off to London early, but she missed him.

Emma walked up to the school, and saw the parents quickly sending children in out of the rain. She usually spoke to people now. She saw Debby wave to her, but she couldn't bear to talk to anyone, not today.

Later, she rang her mother, but she had been on her way out. Friends had remembered the date and were taking her out to lunch. People had been very supportive of her mother. Emma was glad for her, but wished she had a brother or sister to talk to, someone who understood how she felt. She had read a book which said that sibling relationships were special, outside the touch of time. She loved that expression. Lizzy was part of the DNA of her life: the past, the present and, she had imagined, she would be there for her future. It was Lizzy who had first come to see Flora when she had been born, been her godparent. Emma had always imagined she would be doing those things for Lizzy one day and that Flora and her cousin would be friends. That future had been snatched away.

Somehow, Emma got through the day, but the sadness ate away inside her.

As they sat eating their evening meal, Flora said, 'It's the puppy class tonight.'

'Oh dear. Maybe next week–'

'No, Mum. We should take Ollie. It would be good for him. Skyler is taking his sister Honey; they can train together.'

There was no way Emma could get out of it; they had to go.

There were about eight puppies in the hall. Ollie was very excited to see Honey.

Debby was a much better teacher here. She stayed calm and was much more organised. Emma thought how much better she was with dogs than with children.

Emma was surprised at how competitive she felt. She wanted Ollie to be the best, quickest, the most obedient. Of course, he wasn't: far from it. He pulled on the lead trying to get to Honey. He barked at the other dogs, stood when he was meant to sit, and looked at everything other than her when they did 'watch me'. By the time he went to wee over another puppy during the play time Emma was close to tears.

Then they came to the recall. Emma had to leave Ollie, walk a number of steps, then call him. When she called him, he completely ignored her. She tried again, but it got no better. The experience was made worse by the fact that they had to do this individually in turn and every other puppy had done it right. Emma called, but to no effect. Everyone was watching her.

She felt Flora tugging her jumper. 'Mum, stop crying.' Emma, who hadn't realised that she was, quickly wiped her face.

Debby walked Ollie back to her and said quietly, 'We'll chat after.'

Emma felt herself go red: as with everything here she had failed.

Everyone else left in good spirits, shouting thanks and goodbyes to Debby. For a brief moment Emma hated them all.

'You girls can sweep the floor and play with the puppies. I need to go over here and talk to Emma,' said Debby.

She came over and sat next to Emma on a plastic chair.

'What's the matter?' asked Debby.

'I'm just useless at this.'

'No. Your heart wasn't in it tonight. Dogs know. You weren't interested, so why should he be?'

'I'm sorry.'

'You didn't look right this morning. Is something wrong?'

Emma sat back and shook her head.

'I know I'm loud, but I'm not a gossip,' said Debby. 'You haven't looked happy since you came to Ruxton. Do you hate it here? Don't worry. I can understand. It's hardly the most glamorous place.'

'It's not this place, honestly. It's something that happened just before we came.'

'Were you ill?'

'No.'

'What, then?'

'Nothing.'

'Emma, you need to talk. What happened?'

'Someone died.' The words came out too hard, brutal.

'I'm sorry. Who was it that you lost?'

Emma took a deep breath. 'It was my sister.'

'Oh no. What was the matter? Was she ill?'

'She was hit by a car. Drunk driver. It was so senseless. He died as well. It destroyed my Mum. She was everything to her, you see.'

'How is your Mum now?'

'Coping. People have rallied round. Some friends took her out for lunch today. It would have been Lizzy's birthday.'

'But no one took you out?'

'Of course not.'

Debby nodded. 'We are the forgotten ones, you know: brothers, sisters of those who died; we get forgotten. We look after everyone, but we have lost as well.'

Emma looked at Debby intently. Between their gaze there was a thin thread of understanding. 'You actually know what I am talking about, don't you?' she whispered.

Debby nodded. 'Skyler's mother, my younger sister. She died as well.'

'Oh no. How?'

'She overdosed at a party. She wasn't an addict. It was just the once, some dodgy tablets.'

'That's awful.'

'It was. But, you know, at first I was so angry. I didn't tell anyone, but it was how I felt.'

'Why?'

'Because she'd left me with sick parents and now a baby to look after. She'd never been very responsible. I mean, she got pregnant young and, even after Skyler was born, she was off partying. I had finally saved up and got a place to do animal care at college. I would be older than the other students, but I didn't mind. Then she had her accident. I had to give it up. I know it sounds selfish, but it was always me, you see, who looked after everyone. When she'd gone, I missed her like crazy, but I was angry.'

Emma bit her lip. 'I get angry, you know. Not for the same reason, though.'

'Why, then?'

'Because my Mum goes on all the time how much Flora is like Lizzy. I can see it, but it's such a burden. Mum is always saying I should be stretching her more. Of course, she is pleased we are moving somewhere–' Emma stopped.

'Somewhere posher?'

'You could say that… and I thought it was the right thing for Flora, although she suddenly seems to be settling now. She loves the beach, and getting Ollie has been a big help. The trouble is, I don't think I really fit here.'

The words hung in the air. Emma waited for Debby to say, 'No. It's a shame but you don't, not really.' However, she noticed that Debby had gone red. 'I'm sorry. I haven't helped, have I?'

'I was tactless. You know, over the coffee and things,' admitted Emma.

'I guess this place means a lot to me. My standing here: you see, it's all I have. I've not done much work-wise. People respect me here. And you, well, to be honest, when I saw your shoes and clothes, I thought, 'Well, she's not going to stick it here.' A lot of people come and go, you know. They come, thinking they are going to save us all, but give them a few dreary winters and they leave.'

Emma heard the hurt in her voice. 'I'm sorry.'

'It's OK. Can't blame them. I thought you were just like the others.'

'I was numb really. Maybe I should have said something.'

'We'd have understood better. You just seemed a bit off. Still, I put you in a pigeon-hole, and it wasn't fair.'

Debby looked over at the girls playing. 'They get on well, don't they?'

'Yes, they do.'

'Maybe we should try to get on better?'

Emma nodded. 'That would be good.'

'You know, I was thinking that if you wanted to take on the Sunday group, well until you go, I wouldn't mind.'

'Really?'

'I saw your face when Flora gave you the picture on Sunday.'

Emma cringed. 'Sorry.'

'That's OK. To be honest, I'm much happier with my dogs than the kids.'

They both laughed.

'I've been asked to do some more dog training classes, and sometimes I would need to be available on a Sunday. I could do that, at least until you go.'

'I'd like that. You might find some of the shows are on a Sunday as well?'

'Yes, I thought of that. But that's in the future. When you go, I can guarantee no-one else will take the group on. And, you see, I don't want Skyler to miss out on church. She meets nice kids here. I want to do the best for her, you know.'

'I understand. We all want that for our children.'

Emma looked over at Flora, who was now quietly instructing Ollie to do the perfect sit and recall.

Debby stood up. 'I'm sorry we got off on the wrong foot. If you changed your mind and decided to stay, it would be really good for us all.'

Emma stood next to her. 'Thank you. It's really helped to talk to someone who understands.'

Later that evening, Chris returned from his meeting very excited. 'We're going to get the money. It's amazing. The MP came. She's been working so hard behind the scenes. I hate to say this but, because the statistics for health and education around here are so awful, it worked in our favour. Apparently, we are to become what they are calling a 'beacon town', like a place to try out new ideas. It's very exciting. I shall at least feel like I'm leaving something good here.'

'Would you like to stay and see it through?'

Chris looked puzzled. 'Of course, but–'

'The other job: is it too late to pull out of it?'

Chris frowned at her. 'I wouldn't have thought so. Although they would have people queuing up for it and, of course, there've been no applications for down here yet.'

'So we could stay?'

'Hang on. Have you changed your mind suddenly? What about Flora?'

'I think Flora will be OK. She has us, a school where she is happy, and, of course, Ollie and the beach.'

'Your Mum wouldn't like it.'

'I know. It's hard, but we need to let Flora be herself. It's too much for us and certainly too much for Flora for her to be forced into being someone else. She needs to be free.'

Ollie started to scratch at the back door. Emma and Chris took him outside and stood close together under the umbrella, waiting. Emma felt the water soaking into her shoes.

Chris hugged her. 'Are you alright about staying? Seriously, I know what you've been through.'

'I am. Really, I would like to make a fresh start. Well, on one proviso.'

'What's that?'

'That I can go to the shops tomorrow and buy a decent pair of wellington boots.'

102

If you have enjoyed these short stories you may be interested in this taster of Mary Grand's second novel, "Hidden Chapters", published in August 2016. Here are the first two chapters.

Hidden Chapters

Chapter One

Saturday 30th July 1994

'I've found the girl,' shouted Catrin in panic, her hands shaking as she shone her torch down on the crumpled body. She stepped over the soaking headland grass, reached down and touched the girl's frozen hand.

'Gareth' she called, but her words were drowned by the rain and the sound of the waves crashing on the rocks of Rhossili Bay far below. To the left of the headland path was a fence and fields, but the girl lay on the other side of the path where a grassy area led to the treacherous unprotected cliff edge.

'Come over here!' She screamed to Gareth. To her relief she saw him turn his torch her way. He left the path and came slowly towards her. Gareth knelt down beside the girl, feeling for a pulse. He pushed her long wet hair away from her face.

'She's unconscious,' he shouted to Catrin. The sodden, thin, white, smock dress clung to the girl. As

Gareth shone his torch down her body, Catrin saw the neat bump, which had been disguised earlier at the party.

'We must get an ambulance, and quickly,' said Gareth. 'Where the hell is your brother? Where's Aled?'

'I don't know,' Catrin cried, tears now mingling with the rain on her face.

Out of the darkness, a calm detached voice asked, 'Something up?'

Catrin shone her torch beam up and wiped the rain out of her eyes. She saw a man clothed in waterproofs, carrying fishing tackle. He was walking along the path from the direction of the causeway which linked the headland to the island of Worm's Head. Catrin assumed he had been fishing off the rocks by the causeway.

'This girl has fallen,' Gareth shouted. 'She needs an ambulance.'

'Oh, right,' said the man, almost casually. 'I could go and call for one from the hotel up there.'

'Great. Tell them it's urgent. The girl is heavily pregnant.'

Catrin stood up. 'Did you see anyone on your way back here?'

'Yeah. A fellow ran past me. He seemed to be heading to the causeway. I shouted to come back. It's getting bloody dangerous out there tonight. I don't know whether heard me, but he didn't stop.'

'Is the causeway covered by the sea at the moment?'

'Not yet, but the tide will be coming in soon.'

'Catrin, this girl needs an ambulance,' interrupted Gareth. He looked up at the fisherman. 'Please, can you go now?'

'Right, I'm off,' said the fisherman, and he disappeared into the darkness.

At that moment, Catrin heard a feeble voice from the girl. She leant down.

'It's alright. We're here to help you.'

'Where's Aled?' The girl started to cry quietly.

'I don't know,' said Catrin. She stared through the darkness in the direction of the causeway and looked down at the girl. 'Don't worry, I'll go and find him.'

Gareth grabbed her arm. 'You're not to go anywhere. It's treacherous out here. Aled's not a child. He won't do anything stupid.'

'I have to go. Maybe he's lost his sense of direction. It's so confusing out here in the pitch black. Anything could happen.'

'That's why you shouldn't go.'

'Don't worry, I've got a torch, and I'll keep close to the fence,' Catrin said, adding, 'You're the doctor; you have to stay with the girl.' Before Gareth could stop her, Catrin left.

She clung to the fence to stop herself from wandering towards the cliff edge. She was soaked through and shivering now. The rain felt like sharp pins. It was hurting her face. Eventually she reached the coastguard's hut situated at the top of the steep incline which led down to the causeway. In the distance she could make out specks of angry white foam on the peaks of the waves. She pointed her torch down towards the muddy, stony path, then further on to the causeway. She could just make out some rocks, but the sea was slowly devouring the crossing. Catrin screamed out for Aled. There was no reply, so she started to clamber down the slippery path. Catrin managed a few steps but, as she looked up to scream Aled's name again, she lost her footing, fell forwards, and started to tumble out of control down the bank. She dropped the torch, which smashed on to a rock. Catrin tried desperately to grab at wet tufts of grass, but kept tumbling down, until she crashed into a large boulder which saved her from falling into the gathering torrent below. Petrified, she clung to the rock. She pulled herself up to a sitting position, but continued to hold on. She daren't move for fear of falling again. She knew that the strong currents of the sea covering the causeway would claim even the strongest swimmer. Her right arm, which had caught the main force of the collision with the rock, was throbbing. The pain was excruciating. Catrin just stayed there, hanging on desperately, waiting. She was just starting to despair of anyone coming when she heard her name, and recognised Gareth's voice shouting through the darkness.

'I'm here,' she shouted back. 'Be careful: it's really slippery.'

A powerful light blinded her, and a man in a reflective jacket came and pulled her up the slope. Gareth was waiting, grabbed hold of her and held her close.

'What the hell are you doing? You could have been killed,' he exclaimed.

'I can't find him.' Catrin pulled away from his grasp and shouted hysterically. 'I kept calling. I don't know where he is.'

'You have to come away. It's not safe.'

'I can't. I can't go back without him.'

'This man is with the search and rescue. They'll take over now,' said Gareth.

'No. I can't go back. Not without Aled. My parents will never forgive me.'

'Don't be stupid. The people here have enough to do looking for Aled, without worrying about you,' responded Gareth sharply.

Catrin had to give in, and allowed Gareth and the man to take her back along the headland, through the gate, into the car park. She saw a police car. A police officer walked towards her

'Where's the girl?' she asked Gareth.

'She's gone in an ambulance,' he said. 'I couldn't tell them anything about her. I gave them your parents' phone number.'

The policeman shone his torch on the gash on her right arm. Catrin saw for the first time that her coat was torn and that her arm was covered in blood.

'You look cold,' said the police officer. 'What's the matter with that arm?'

'It's nothing. I'll sort it out.'

'That needs stitching,' said Gareth.

'No. I have to get back to The Dragon House, to Mum and Dad; tell them what is happening.' Catrin heard a helicopter. She saw the spotlights on the surface of the water, which only emphasised the vast area of black unsearched sea surrounding them. Where was her Aled? Nothing made sense. The one thing she knew was that they had to find him.

Chapter Two

Whoever said time heals all wounds is a liar, thought Catrin. Eighteen years: wasn't that long enough? She thought she had recovered well, but actually being forced to return to Gower was like tearing off the plaster and finding that nothing had healed.

When her father Lloyd had told her he was planning to sell The Dragon House she had been hugely relieved. The house had been abandoned since Aled's accident. No-one had visited it, but she had known it was there: empty and looking resentful. Then her father had asked Bethan, her daughter, to go for two weeks to help sort the house out ready for it to be sold. Catrin had been shocked. She had assumed her father would get in house clearance. No-one wanted to go back there. However, her father had been determined to sort it out himself and do some decorating. He said that no way would he get the asking price otherwise. Again, Catrin had been dumbfounded that her father, who was comfortable financially, was prepared to go back just to make money. Bethan, who was determined to go, had been excited. Knowing her mother's reluctance, she had said that as she was nearly eighteen she would go alone. This was difficult. There would be some very sensitive conversations to be had down there. Catrin was sure that her father did not have the ability to handle them, and in a sense, there was no logical reason for Catrin not to go. She had a long summer off work ahead of her, with no major commitments. Maybe she should help her father? She was starting to weaken, when her father told her that he was planning to hold a memorial service for Aled at

108

Rhossili Church during those weeks and that he was having a bench placed in the churchyard in his memory. At this point, Catrin finally relented: her visit to Gower was unavoidable. It was decided that they would travel down on the Saturday before the memorial.

And so it happened that Catrin and Bethan were stuck in holiday traffic heading out of Cardiff towards Gower. The sun was burning Catrin's right arm through the cotton sleeve which covered the long white scar on her arm. On the back seat lay folded cardboard boxes and empty cases and bin bags. Glancing in the mirror, Catrin could see a woman in the car behind tapping her fingers on the steering wheel in time to some music, while her children on the back seat were looking down at screens. Catrin envied their calm, their normality. Bethan touched Catrin gently on the arm and Catrin turned to face her.

They communicated together using speech and signs. Bethan had been born Deaf. She had some residual hearing and, with the best hearing aids and speech teaching, she had learned to speak. Gareth and Catrin also believed that Bethan should grow up feeling part of the Deaf community. The family learned to sign, albeit they only signed in the order of spoken language. Bethan was fluent in British Sign Language, which had its own grammar and syntax. She loved to use it when she was socialising with her local Deaf friends. Bethan chose always to describe herself as being Deaf with a capital D.

'I know you don't want to go to Gower,' Bethan said, her signing as well as her voice reflecting her conviction. 'I know that you hate it there, but I think it will be good for us to go.'

'It's not that I hate it–' Catrin started to answer.

'For God's sake, Mum. Why haven't you been back before, then?'

'It's complicated.'

'That's what you always say. It doesn't make sense. The accident was years ago. Anyway, I'm really excited. I'll finally see The Dragon House, the beach, and, of course,' she paused, 'Worm's Head.'

Catrin bit her lip hard and Bethan, seeing her, tutted in irritation. 'Honestly, Mum, you should have moved on by now.'

Catrin looked away. What did people expect? She had carried on with her life, hadn't she? In fact, in the past eighteen years she had brought up her two beautiful girls and it had been the most fulfilling time of her life. It was just that, somehow, the ghosts of that night never went away. They were always there whispering over her shoulder.

'It's not that easy,' she said.

'Well, you only have to go this once. The Dragon House will be sold soon and you'll never have to come again. Is the house in a real state? No-one has been there to stay since the accident have they?'

'Grandad has had cleaners going in. I don't think it's too bad. I just wish he'd sold it sooner.'

'He said he knew it would increase in value if he waited.'

'Yes, he told me that, but it's not like he's short of money. I understood why he couldn't sell straight after Aled died. None of us could think straight then. My mother would have found it hard to let go of the house. After all, it might have just been a holiday home for them by then, but it was where she was brought up. I did think Dad would have sold it after she died, but he kept insisting it would go up in value.'

'And he was right.'

'He was in a sense. It's worth a lot now, apparently.'

'He thinks this is finally the right moment to sell then?'

110

'Well, you know, he has decided to move to New York permanently. I think he's decided it's time.'

'He's very old to be moving all that way, isn't he?'

Catrin grinned. 'Don't say that to Grandad. He's always telling me seventy is the new, I don't know, fifty or something. Anyway, he's spent so much time there over the years I guess it's not such a big thing. He has a lot of friends over there and a flat. In some ways I'm surprised he's waited so long to move out there.'

'What will he do with his proper home in Cardiff?'

'I don't know. Your Grandad doesn't tell me much. We'll have to ask him, won't we?'

'You used to have holidays at The Dragon House before Aled's accident, didn't you?'

'Oh yes. When I was little, when my Mother's Mum, my Nana Beth, was alive, we had wonderful holidays there. Rhossili Bay is an amazing place. It's been voted one of the most beautiful beaches in the world, but it's so much more than that. Everywhere is stuffed with ancient history. You know, they found a skeleton in a cave close to Rhossili which is something like thirty three thousand years old. Can you imagine that? On the beach there are old wrecks sticking up through the sand. There are standing stones on the downs, and there are all these stories of ghosts, pirates and smugglers. It's an extraordinary place.'

'And there's Worm's Head,' interrupted Bethan.

Catrin stopped speaking.

'I want to see it. Go there, you know,' said Bethan.

Catrin glanced at Bethan and saw that screwed-up, determined look she had seen on her daughter's face so many times. That determination had sparked plenty of family rows but had also played an important part in Bethan's ability to cope so well with life. A teacher had said to Catrin when Bethan was still at preschool, 'Never limit what Bethan can do. She can achieve anything she wants.' The years since had been a journey with many tears

111

as well as triumphs, but it had been Bethan's determination that had been one of the most important factors in her thriving. Bethan loved music and tried to explain to people that music was so much more that just an auditory experience. She had amazed teachers by not only learning to play the flute but attaining distinction in her exams. She had been offered an unconditional place to study music at Cardiff University in September.

The car in front moved. Catrin inched forward. She and Bethan didn't tend to attempt to converse while Catrin was driving. It was usually an easy silence. However, today Catrin could not relax, and instead was trying desperately to stay calm. 'Two weeks, and the visit will be over,' she kept repeating to herself like a mantra.

The car ground to a halt again. Catrin breathed slowly and started to feel her pounding heart slow down.

Oblivious to her mother's discomfort, Bethan started chatting again, her voice calmer, and signing more relaxed.

'Sabrina and I were watching the opening of the Olympic Games last night.'

'Oh really? I'm sorry I missed it. Was it good?' Catrin answered, thinking the conversation had moved on. But, of course, it hadn't.

'They showed Rhossili Bay.'

'Really? Are you sure it was Rhossili?'

'Oh yes. I read it on the subtitles.'

'How come it was in the ceremony?'

'They had a film of these kids in T shirts singing on the beach. You and Dad should have seen it.'

'I was busy trying to write this article about Aled for Grandad.'

'What's that for then?'

'He wants me to write something for the firm's website about Aled, to put up after the memorial. It's difficult. I'm not sure how many people will even remember him. I guess if it's for the website I need to write about Aled as an architect. I know he was meant to be outstanding at his work, but I don't know any details. It makes me realise how little I actually know about Aled in the years before he died, most of which he spent working in America. We hardly ever communicated then whether by letter or phone. He didn't even come over to my wedding. The night of his accident was the first time I'd seen him for about three years. It's a chapter of his life I know very little about.'

'Well, anyway,' continued Bethan, not interested in her mother's dilemma, 'about Worm's Head. I said we saw it on TV. Sabrina said it didn't look anything like a worm. What is it like there? Why's it called that?'

Despite the heat in the car, Catrin shivered. She was there. She could feel the wind burning her cheeks as she peered into pitch blackness, the driving rain mingled with tears on her face.

As she sat in the car, Catrin suddenly felt her heart start to pound. Oh God, not now, not a panic attack. She consciously slowed her breathing, counted silently, then she tried to notice the things around her: the hot sticky steering wheel clenched by her fingers; the sweat running down her back; the heat of the sun on her arm; and, out there, a buzzard hovering just at the edge of the motorway.

'You alright, Mum?'

'Yes, I'm fine.'

'So why is it called Worm's Head?'

'Let me think. Yes, the name comes from a very old Viking word, w-u-r-m (she finger spelled), which actually means Dragon. The story goes that Vikings were invading Rhossili on a foggy night and they thought Worm's Head was a dragon.'

'So really it should be called Dragon's Head? Wow. Is that why Grandad's house is called The Dragon House?'

113

'That's right. The Dragon House is actually in a tiny village called Bryn Draig. It's up from Rhossili on the side of the downs. You can see Worm's Head from there.'

'And it was on Worm's Head that Aled fell? On TV I saw it was an island, so how did he get there? Was he in a boat or something?'

Catrin gritted her teeth. This was one of the reasons going back was such a mistake, and particularly to go with Bethan. She was bound to be full of questions, questions Catrin couldn't answer, talk that would stir up memories best forgotten. If it had been simply her and her father it would have been easier. They both knew the boundaries of what they would talk about. Bethan was like a small child running around a silent church picking up sacred things and shouting out questions. Even the way she said Aled's name was all wrong. The correct way to say it was in solemn, reverent tones. Also, the accident was not something to be glibly talked about. If it had to be mentioned, you skirted tactfully around it, spoke hesitantly, embarrassed to have brought it up. However, Bethan had no idea of this unspoken etiquette. Catrin coughed and tried to answer her.

'Worm's Head is not always cut off. There's a strip of land, a causeway that links Worm's Head to the mainland. Most of the time it is covered with sea, but for a few hours each day it is clear.'

'Do you mean like that place we went in France where the monastery was?'

'M-o-n-t-S-a-i-n-t-M-i-c-h-e-l?' Catrin finger spelled. 'That's it.'

'Yes, something like that, but there is no man-made path. It's a very rough causeway, and on Worm's Head there are no buildings. No-one lives there, well, apart from sheep. People do visit via the causeway when it's open.'

'So Aled went over the causeway? It sounds an exciting place. It must have been fun going over when you were younger. You know, when you went to stay at The Dragon House when you were little.'

'Actually, I've never been to Worm's Head. My mother, your Grandma Isabel, was adamant we should never go there, so we never did.'

'But Aled went on the night of his party?'

Catrin nodded. 'Yes, but no-one knows why.'

'It wasn't a birthday party for Aled, was it? I mean, he was pretty old by then?'

'Aled was only twenty seven, but, no. It wasn't a birthday party. My parents were celebrating him coming to work in Grandad's practice. Aled had been out in New York for about three years working in an associated office. Grandad was very excited he was coming back.'

'I'd have thought it was a bit of a come down to come back to the UK from America.'

Catrin fiddled with her bracelet. 'Aled was going to head up some big project here. He was an outstanding architect.'

'Grandad is always telling me that.'

'Aled was very special.' The car in front made a move and Catrin turned away to concentrate on driving.

Eventually they were able to leave the motorway and turn off towards Swansea. Catrin saw the first brown sign to Gower. She really was going there. Soon it will all be over, she reminded herself and, as a further distraction, she started to try and plan the things she would do after the visit. The garden: that's what she would do. She would have a go at the border; pull out the bindweed that was taking over.

Then she gripped the steering wheel. That was exactly what she had been thinking eighteen years ago as she and Gareth had driven to Gower for Aled's party. She had been nervous about going then, though, on reflection, the reasons seemed relatively trivial. The thing was that she had not been married long then, and had hated leaving her first child Lowri. It was their first night apart. She remembered giving Gareth's parents numerous lists, clothes and equipment for every possible eventuality, but still she had been worried. But, of course, there had been no question of them not going: the party was for Aled. However, she had been dreading the whole thing. Socialising with her father's trendy architect friends always made her feel so inadequate. Also, of course, her mother would be there. Catrin always worried about her at social occasions. She remembered sitting in the car next to Gareth on the way to the party her hands clasped together, thinking, 'Get through tonight; we can leave straight after breakfast. I can go home and have a good go at the garden.'

But that's not what had happened. She had sleepwalked into one of the most momentous, life-changing moments of her life. Back in Cardiff in those days she had an enormous family calendar on which she kept meticulous record of all the events coming up. It had made her feel in control of her life. But that night things had happened which demonstrated that that was a complete illusion. The calendar had been torn up on her return. Nothing had been the same since the night of the thirtieth of July nineteen-ninety-four.

As she drove now to Gower with Bethan, and planned her time after the visit, she reassured herself that fate would never do that to her again: lightning never strikes in the same place twice. She sat back and tried to relax, tried to silence the voices that nagged away, telling her that she was wrong. Because, of course, deep down she knew that lightning can strike more than once in the same place and, if that could happen, surely fate could catch her again, could once more set in motion events for which she was totally unprepared. Once again, events could occur that would change her life and the lives of those around her, for ever.

If you would like to read on, you will find "Hidden Chapters" at Amazon as a paperback and an ebook.

To be notified as soon as my next book is published, or to send feedback, please send an email to marygrand90@yahoo.co.uk

If you have liked "Making Changes" please take the time to post a short review. It really makes a difference in encouraging others to have a look at it. Thank you.

Find me at https://marygrand.net/ on facebook @authormarygrand or follow me on twitter @authormaryg

Mary Grand

About the Author

I was born in Cardiff and have retained a deep love for my Welsh roots. I worked as a nursery teacher in London and later taught Deaf children in Croydon and Hastings.

I now live on the beautiful Isle of Wight with my husband, where I walk my cocker spaniel Pepper and write. I have two grown up children.

I have written three novels, 'Free to Be Tegan' and 'Hidden Chapters', set in Wales, and 'Behind the Smile' set on the Isle of Wight. I have also published a previous book of short stories 'Catching the Light' which is also available as an audio book narrated by Petrina Kingham.

Printed in Great Britain
by Amazon